D

As Henry stumbled towards the stage, the audience clapped its hands, stamped its feet, cheered and whistled through its fingers. Henry blinked in the glare of the spotlight which seemed to be following him everywhere.

There was a short flight of steps at one side of the theatre leading up on to the stage. The old man crossed and leaned over, coaxing Henry up to join him. Then, taking the boy gently by the hand, the old man led him across to the very centre of the stage.

The drum-roll stopped with a flourish.

This time the silence in the theatre was absolute. Henry, his hand still in the old man's grip, gazed out into the sea of faces that were staring back at him, and wondered what his parents had landed him in this time . . .

DRAGON DAYS
Willis Hall

Illustrated by
Alison Claire Darke

RED FOX

A Red Fox Book

Published by Random House Children's Books
20 Vauxhall Bridge Road, London SW1V 2SA

A division of Random House UK Ltd
London Melbourne Sydney Auckland
Johannesburg and agencies throughout the world

1 3 5 7 9 10 8 6 4 2

First published by The Bodley Head 1985

Red Fox edition 1995

Papers used by Random House UK Limited
are natural, recyclable products made from wood grown in
sustainable forests. The manufacturing processes conform to
the environmental regulations of the country of origin.

Printed and bound in Great Britain by
Cox & Wyman Ltd, Reading, Berkshire

RANDOM HOUSE UK Limited Reg. No. 954009

ISBN 0 09 911581 6

I

The old man in the magician's costume made several magic passes over the top hat with his long, thin fingers, then plunged his hand inside and pulled out a grey and grubby-looking rabbit.

The audience applauded.

The old man smiled. He dipped his hand into the hat again and this time drew out a long string of flags of all nations.

The audience stamped its feet.

The old man paused. The moons and stars on his gown and pointed hat twinkled, mysteriously. His smile broadened as he beamed out at the stalls and then up into the circle. Suddenly, he slipped his hand into the top hat yet again and this time produced a huge bouquet of feathery flowers.

The audience cheered and whistled through its fingers.

The old man held up his outstretched hands for silence. He walked down to the front of the stage and peered out over the footlights. "Ladies and gentlemen," he began, "for my next miracle, I shall require the assistance of one small boy."

There were a few moments of respectful silence, broken only by the crinkling of potato-crisp packets and the rustle of toffee-papers.

"Come along," said the old man in the magician's costume, "surely there is a small boy somewhere in the audience who is willing to come up here and help me?"

Mrs Emily Hollins, sitting in the third row of the stalls, nudged her eleven-year-old son sharply in the ribs. "Go on, Henry—*you* put your hand up," she urged. "Don't be shy!"

"He who hesitates is lost," observed Albert Hollins, Henry's father, who was sitting on the boy's other side.

Henry shook his head, closed his eyes, shrank down in his seat and wished he were somewhere else.

"I'll do it, mister!" called out a bold lad from the back of the stalls. A number of the audience turned in their seats and craned their necks to see where the voice had come from.

"And me!" yelled another brave spirit, emboldened by the first.

"Me!" "Me, mister!" "I will!" And now adventurous boys were volunteering from all parts of the theatre.

The old man put his hand up above his head and stuck out a skinny forefinger. This was the cue for a steady, regular drum-roll from the drummer in the orchestra pit. As the drum-roll continued, the stabbing beam of a spotlight from somewhere overhead roved around the audience, row after row. Whilst young boys' arms waved about, wildly, in all parts of the theatre, the wandering beam of the spotlight came to a stop on seat number 23 in the third row of the stalls.

Henry Hollins, dazzled by the beam, screwed up his eyes and tried to curl up, even smaller, in his seat.

"I'll take that boy there!" called out the old man in the magician's costume.

Emily Hollins smiled at Henry's side. "There's no getting out of it now," she whispered to her son. "His mind's made up. He wants you."

"It is a far, far better thing you do now," chuckled Albert Hollins, "than you have ever done before!" With which, he took hold of Henry's wrist and, helping him up on to his feet, directed him out into the aisle.

As Henry stumbled towards the stage, the audience clapped its hands, stamped its feet, cheered and whistled through its fingers. Henry blinked in the glare of the spotlight which seemed to be following him everywhere.

There was a short flight of steps at one side of the theatre leading up on to the stage. The old man crossed and leaned over, coaxing Henry up to join him. Then, taking the boy gently by the hand, the old man led him across to the very centre of the stage.

The drum-roll stopped with a flourish.

This time the silence in the theatre was absolute. Henry, his hand still in the old man's grip, gazed out into the sea of faces that were staring back at him, and wondered what his parents had landed him in this time . . .

It had begun one evening, several months before, when Albert Hollins had laid down his knife and fork, importantly, and made an announcement across the dinner table. "I've got a great idea for our holidays this year," he had said.

Emily and Henry had exchanged a worried glance. They had heard some of Albert's "great ideas" before. Particularly with regard to holidays. The Hollins family's holidays never seemed to turn out quite the way they were intended.

"Go on, we're listening," said Emily, with a wink at Henry. "What have you got lined up for us this time? A fun-packed fortnight hobnobbing with the rich and famous on the golden beaches of the French Riviera? Or two weeks water-skiing and skin-diving in the clear blue Caribbean seas?"

"Neither of those," said Albert. "I was thinking of fourteen days paddling with the poor and penniless in Cockleton-on-Sea."

Emily's face fell. "Not Cockleton-on-Sea again!" she wailed.

"Can't we do something *different* this year?" begged Henry. "We go there every year."

"That's not entirely true," Albert replied. "We have *tried* other places—it's just that there's nowhere *quite* as nice as Cockleton-on-Sea."

8

"We've never tried hobnobbing with the rich and famous on the French Riviera," sighed Emily, despondently.

"*Or* skin-diving in the Caribbean," said Henry. "We *always* end up at Cockleton-on-Sea."

"Staying at the Sea View Private Hotel," added his mother.

"Not this time though," said Albert. "That's my great idea. We're not going to stay in an hotel—this year's going to be different!"

"He's going to get that old tent out again, Henry," said Emily, in horror. "The last time we went on a camping holiday it was *disastrous!*"*

"I do wish you'd let me finish," grumbled Albert with a slow shake of his head. "We're not taking the tent anywhere. I'm borrowing a caravan this year, from Mr Witherspoon at work."

The Hollins family lived in a town called Staplewood where Albert Hollins worked in the office of a factory that made plaster garden gnomes and exported them all over the world. Cyril Witherspoon worked on the factory's production line. However, the news that they were going to spend a holiday in Mr Witherspoon's caravan did not appear to overjoy either Emily or Henry.

Henry Hollins looked doubtful.

Emily Hollins sniffed. "Will it be *all right*?" she asked.

"Of course it'll be 'all right'," snapped Albert. "Cyril Witherspoon is regarded as one of the finest garden-gnome craftsmen in the world. He'd hardly lend us his caravan if it

* Anyone wondering how disastrous the Hollins' camping holiday had been can read about this adventure in another Henry Hollins' book: *The Last Vampire.*

wasn't *all right*, would he now?" Albert paused, and added: "It'll be more than *all* right—you'll see—it'll be *great!*"

And Albert had spoken so convincingly that neither Emily nor Henry felt disposed to argue with him.

When holiday-time came round, the caravan had been delivered by Mr Witherspoon, attached to the back of the Hollins' car, and towed all the way to Cockleton-on-Sea. The caravan site, they discovered, was ideal, high up and overlooking the sea.

And, after the first few days, Henry Hollins was ready to admit that both caravan and holiday were better than *all right*.

They had netted shrimps in the soft, wet sand at the water's edge.

They had played beach-cricket using their coats for stumps and Henry had clean-bowled Albert and scored seventeen off one over of Emily's leg-break bowling.

They had eaten candy-floss and fish-and-chips and ice-cream cones and hot-dogs-with-onions-and-mustard and syrupy waffles and hamburgers-with-relish and freshly fried sugary doughnuts—though not all at once.

And, in the dark of late evening, they had strolled along the empty beach, under the stars, listened to the tide slapping beneath the pier, looked out at the tiny fishing boats as they bobbed at anchor, and smelled the tang of the sea carried in on the breeze.

Henry Hollins, in fact, would have told you himself that it had been a *perfect* holiday—right up to the moment when he found himself on the stage of the South Pier Theatre, gazing out at that terrifying sea of faces . . .

The old man in the magician's costume put an arm around Henry's shoulders and smiled down at him. "What's your name, boy?"

"Henry."

"*Just* Henry?" asked the old man, stroking his long beard. "Or is there more of it?"

"Henry Hollins," muttered Henry.

"He says his name is Henry Hollins!" The old man's voice boomed out across the theatre as far as the usherette who was standing at the very back of the stalls, clutching a tray of orange drinks and choc-ices and waiting for the interval. "And tell me, Master Hollins," continued the old man, "do you take this with you *everywhere* you go?" As he spoke, the old man's fingers danced at the side of Henry's face and he pulled an egg out of the boy's ear.

The audience hooted with laughter.

In the third row of the stalls, Emily Hollins turned to Albert. "I don't think he had an egg in his ear when we came out of that café after lunch," she whispered, adding, "I'm sure I'd have noticed if he had."

"It was probably up the old man's sleeve," Albert whispered back.

Up on the stage, the old man performed a few more mystical passes. "And tell me, young Master Hollins, is this yours too?" he asked, pulling a brilliantly coloured large silk handkerchief out of Henry's other ear.

"And I know for a certain fact *that* wasn't there at lunchtime," whispered Emily, "because I had to give him a paper hanky to blow his nose."

As the audience's gales of laughter rang in his ears, Henry Hollins wished that the stage might open and swallow him up.

The old man in the curious costume held up his hands for silence. "Ladies and gentlemen, with the assistance of my young friend, I am about to attempt a feat of magic that will astound and mystify you all!" He paused and smiled a secretive smile across the footlights. "Before your very eyes," the old man went on, "I am about to make Master Hollins vanish into thin air!"

The audience gasped.

Henry gulped. He wondered whether he would encounter any difficulty breathing in "thin air"? And whether, if he was going to be invisible to the audience, he would also be invisible to himself?

The old man, who had crossed to the dark recesses at the

back of the stage, now wheeled forward a strange black upright box decorated with magical signs. The box, which was on wheels, was about two metres high and a metre wide.

"Observe the magical cabinet," said the old man, wheeling the box around in a complete circle for the audience's benefit. "You will perceive that there is a door at the front and that there is no other way in, or out, on any of the other three sides." As he spoke, the old man opened the door of the box and rapped on each of the three inside walls with his magician's wand. "May I also draw your attention," he continued, "to the fact that you can see right underneath the cabinet, proving that there are no trapdoors or trickeries in the the cabinet's floor."

The audience murmured its assent. As far as its members were concerned, there was no jiggery-pokery whatsoever about the strange black box.

Once again, the old man lifted a bony forefinger and the drummer began a long and regular drum-roll.

"And now, Master Hollins," said the old man, turning to Henry, "if you would be so good as to enter my magical cabinet?"

Henry gulped again, blinked, summoned his courage and stepped inside the box. The blackness closed in on him as the old man shut the door.

The lights dimmed on the stage. The audience fell silent; not even a programme rustled. The old man waved his wand, muttered a mysterious incantation, fluttered his bony fingers in the air and then, to everyone's astonishment, flung open the cabinet door to reveal that Henry had disappeared completely. To prove that there was no deception, the old man spun the box round on its wheels, displaying all four sides. There was certainly no sign of Henry—inside the cabinet or out.

"How does he do it?" whispered an awestruck Emily, proffering her husband an Exceedingly Strong Peppermint.

"Search me," Albert whispered with a shake of his head. Emily's peppermints were too strong for Albert's palate. "With mirrors, I should think," he added.

The audience cheered and clapped unsparingly as the orchestra struck up a cheery tune and the old man bowed three times.

The red plush curtain came down swiftly, and then rose at once on a red-nosed comedian in a loud check suit.

The comedian had told three funny stories, one about his dog, one about his mother-in-law and one about his wife, before Emily Hollins turned to Albert with a puzzled frown. "What about our Henry?" she said.

"*What* about him?"

"Where is he?"

"I shouldn't worry," advised Albert. "He's probably being treated to a fizzy drink and a chocolate biscuit behind the scenes. He'll turn up again before the show's over."

"*Ssshhh!*" said a fat man sitting in the row behind them. "I'm trying to hear the jokes!"

"Sorry," murmured Emily, and she too tried her hardest to concentrate on the show.

When the final curtain came down on the matinée performance, and there was still no sign of Henry, Albert and Emily Hollins presented themselves at the manager's office in order to voice their concern.

The theatre manager's name was Reginald Grundy. He was sitting behind an overcrowded desk, wearing a dinner jacket, a black bow-tie, and eating fish-and-chips with his fingers out of the *Cockleton-on-Sea Telegraph and Argus*. He frowned as the Hollinses told their story.

"Are you absolutely *sure* he didn't come out of the box again?" asked Mr Grundy.

"Positive," said Emily, firmly. "We wouldn't be here if he had, would we?"

The manager was forced to acknowledge the truth in this remark. He took a snow-white handkerchief out of his trouser pocket and wiped the grease from his fingers. "The only thing I can suggest," he said, "is that we go backstage and see the magician—if he can't tell us what's happened to your little lad, I don't know who can."

It was a sensible suggestion and Emily and Albert Hollins followed the manager through the empty rows of seats towards the stage. "To tell you the honest truth," he said, as he opened the pass door which led from the front-of-house to the back-stage area, "I'm not at all surprised, in my heart of hearts, that something like this has happened."

"Oh?" said Emily. "Why's that then?" And she clutched nervously at Albert's elbow as they followed the manager across the darkened stage.

"Because I had a feeling there was something fishy about that magician chap."

"Oh dear me," said Albert, as the manager led the way along a dark and dusty passage. "Whatever gave you that impression?"

Mr Grundy shrugged. "The way he turned up at the beginning of this week—out of the blue."

"Isn't he here for the summer season then?" asked Emily.

The manager shook his head. "Not at all. He's only standing in this week for a lady sword-swallower and fire-eater. She's off with a sore throat. I didn't know what I was going to do about filling her spot on the bill. And, blow me, this funny old chap walks into my office on Monday morning and says that he's a magician. I've no idea where he came from."

Emily and Albert exchanged a worried glance.

"Mind you," the manager continued, "I was jolly glad to see him at the time—but, as I say, it comes as no great shock there's been this accident." They had arrived outside a dingy door at the very end of the long, dark corridor. The manager knocked on it three times. "This is his dressing room," he said.

There was no reply. He tried again. "Is there anyone in?" he called, loudly. Again there was no answer.

Emily tried the door knob. "It's locked," she said.

"That presents no problem," said Mr Grundy, taking a bunch of keys out of his pocket. "I've a master-key that fits all the dressing-room locks."

A moment later, the three of them were standing inside the tiny dressing room. Not only was it empty, but there was no sign of it having been occupied at all. The grubby dressing table was devoid of make-up and there were no theatrical costumes visible anywhere.

Mr Grundy threw open the wardrobe door and three wire coat-hangers rattled against each other on the rail. "If you ask me," he said, "the old chap's done a bunk."

"But whatever's become of our Henry?" wailed Emily Hollins.

"Search me," said the theatre manager with a heavy sigh. "This would never have happened, y'know, if the lady sword-swallower hadn't gone down with that sore throat."

2

As the door of the magic cabinet shut tight behind him, Henry Hollins was immediately overcome with fear. He was frightened not only because he was standing in total darkness —and couldn't even see his own fingers when he held them up in front of his face—but also because he could not hear one single sound either from the stage or from the audience. It was as if he had been locked in a noise-proof box—as if, almost, he had been transported to another world . . .

Henry stood stock-still for several moments, not daring to move, accustoming himself to the blackness and the silence. He expected a secret door or panel to open at any moment, and the friendly hand of the old magician, or a stage-hand perhaps, to help him out. But no such hand came to his rescue and Henry began to realize that if he was to escape from the dark and lonely interior of the box, he would have to do it by himself.

He reached out and touched the sides of the cabinet one by one, and found to his amazement that one of the four walls of the box was no longer there—only empty blackness lay in front of him.

Henry swallowed, hard.

There was no way of telling how far the dark passage went—and no way of knowing where it might lead. But if he *was* going to get out, he wouldn't do it by standing still.

He set off, slowly at first, and with his hands stretched out to touch the walls on either side, tentatively placing one foot in front of the other, making little progress.

The further he went, however, the more he gained in confidence. The floor beneath his feet was firm and flat and without obstacles. How far he walked he found it difficult to tell, for there was sense neither of time nor distance in the blackness that surrounded him on all sides. It seemed to Henry as if he had been travelling for *hours* and had covered *miles*, but commonsense told him that this couldn't be so—or could it . . .?

Eventually, it occurred to him that he was no longer moving along a passage at all: the walls on either side were not now smooth to his touch but rough and uneven—almost like rock. And the firm flat floor, it seemed, had given way to hard packed earth. Then, as the first glimmer of light appeared, way up ahead, Henry Hollins' growing suspicions were at last confirmed: it wasn't a passage he was walking through, it was an underground tunnel!

He stumbled onwards, less sure of himself in the growing half-light than he had been in the total blackness, but with the end of the tunnel looming ever nearer his spirits rose and his footsteps quickened.

Whereabouts in Cockleton-on-Sea would he find himself, he wondered? Perhaps the tunnel was taking him gradually upwards and he would come out somewhere near the top of the cliffs and close to the caravan site? He certainly hoped so. He was beginning to feel quite hungry. He felt sure his parents would have left the theatre long before and would be waiting for him now, with his tea prepared, in Mr Witherspoon's caravan.

Suddenly, he took a sharp turn and he realized that he had arrived at the tunnel's end. But as he stepped out of the tunnel he found himself not in the open air, as he had expected, but standing in a large and comfortable cave—a cave in which, it was obvious from its contents, somebody lived.

There was a fire glowing in one corner with a huge cast-iron cauldron smouldering over the flames. There were lots of shelves along one wall and these were stocked with old-fashioned bottles of all shapes and sizes which contained liquids all colours of the rainbow. There was a rough-hewn bed in one corner of the cave and a similarly fashioned table and chair both of which were piled high with enormous leather-bound books. But the only sign of life in the cave was a huge spotted toad which was sitting in the flickering shadows cast by the firelight, croaking quietly and contentedly.

Henry peered around into the darkest recesses of the cave, looking for its human inhabitants. "Hello?" he called, and: "Is there anyone at home?" But there was no reply, save for the green-and-yellow toad which croaked all the louder.

Henry crossed, first of all, to inspect the rows of bottles which looked as if they belonged in an ancient chemist's shop. Most of the bottles had labels on them but these were written either in a hand that was illegible or in a foreign language. Next, he moved over to the table where, after blowing away a

thin layer of dust and several cobwebs, Henry read the title which was displayed in strange lettering across the cover of one of the leather-bound volumes:

MYSTICKAL SPELLS
AND
ANCIENTE MAGICKAL POTIONS

Lastly, Henry went over to the vast cauldron and, standing on tiptoe, gazed at the unappetizing grey-green semi-liquid that was bubbling away inside.

"Do you suffer from warts, boy?"

Henry recognized the voice at once. He turned to find that the old magician had followed him through the tunnel into the cave.

"N-n-no," said Henry.

"You are stricken with a plague of festering boils, perhaps?"

"Of course not!"

"Then that potion is of no use to you whatsoever—although it has also been tried, on occasion, for the palsy and the gout—but never with any marked degree of success." The magician crossed to the bubbling cauldron and stirred at the contents with a ladle which hung by the fireplace. He frowned at the mixture. "Mind you," he said with a sigh, "it was never much good for warts or festering boils either."

It occurred to Henry that there were more important things to be discussed than wart-cures. "Why did you bring me here?" he demanded, and: "And how soon can you get me back to Cockleton-on-Sea again?"

The old man pretended not to hear the question. He thumbed through the leather-bound volume of *Mystickal Spells And Anciente Magickal Potions*. "Do you know," he said at last, tapping at a page of the book with his forefinger, "if I added a sprig of henbane and a lizard's tooth, that mixture might very well ward off witches—particularly if there was a full moon."

"If you don't take me back at once," Henry persisted, "I'll find my own way along the tunnel."

"What tunnel might that be, boy?" said the magician.

Henry glanced across the cave but the opening in the rock-wall seemed to have disappeared completely.

"I realize now where I went wrong," said the magician, running his finger along the thick, black writing in the book. "I should never have tried to drink the stuff. It says here that you're supposed to rub it on the affected area. Are you *quite* sure you haven't got a wart or a boil about your person somewhere? I can't wait to try it out properly."

Henry Hollins shook his head, firmly. "If you won't take me back along the tunnel, I'll just have to find another way home," he said.

The old man pointed to a small wooden door in the wall of the cave. "The outside world is through there," he said, and added as Henry went towards it: "But it won't do you much good—it's a long way back."

"I don't care," said Henry, pausing with his hand on the latch. "I'll find my own way. I'll walk along the sands until I'm back in Cockleton-on-Sea. Which way do I turn? Right or left?"

"You don't," said the old man. "I wasn't talking about *miles* —I mean *years*."

Henry, beginning to lose patience, jerked open the door. The sooner he was on his way the better. But he pulled up short as he gazed outside.

His eyes widened.

His mouth opened.

There was no sign of the sea. The cave was situated halfway up a rocky slope which fell away beneath his feet and led to a green and rolling pastureland that stretched as far as the eye could see. There was not a lane or house or fence in sight. But it was not this glimpse of pleasant countryside that had caused him to blink, twice, and swallow, hard.

Henry's eyes had opened wide at the sight of a knight in gleaming armour and plumed helmet, lance at the ready, astride a dappled horse and cantering across his line of vision.

23

His jaw had dropped open as he observed the buttressed walls and many battlements of a tall castle that stood gleaming in the afternoon sun not half a mile from where he stood. The portcullis was raised. The drawbridge was lowered. Thin triangular pennants drifted lazily in the breeze from the top of every turret. Henry, wondering if he was dreaming, watched as the knight urged his caparisoned steed towards the castle. He heard its hooves clatter across the drawbridge planking.

"My name is Merlin," said the old man who had joined Henry at the door of the cave. He put an arm around the boy's shoulder and pointed across at the towering walls. "Welcome to Camelot," he said.

Emily Hollins opened the door of the caravan, looked inside and called back to Albert who was close on her heels. "He's not in here," she said.

Albert Hollins did not reply immediately. Puffing and panting, he followed Emily into the caravan and sank down, heavily, on the dining banquette.

They had walked up from the promenade. It had been a long, slow climb and Albert had carried the bulging beach-bag containing all their swimming things *and* a carrier full of groceries that Emily had paused to pick up on the way. The heavy carrier-bag clanked, noisily, as he put it down on the dining table.

"I don't know why you had to buy so many tins of cat-food," he grumbled at last, "particularly as we haven't got a blinking cat!"

"I got them for that black-and-white stray that's been

miaowing under the caravan every night," she told him. "If we don't feed the poor thing, nobody else will. Anyway, we've got more on our plate than cat-food at the moment. What I want to know is, what's happened to our Henry?"

Albert shook his head, slowly. "It's a mystery to me," he said. "I suppose he'll turn up though, when he's good and ready. It isn't the first time he's gone missing for the afternoon."

"It's the first time he's gone missing in a magic cabinet," Emily pointed out. "I do think we ought to do *something*."

Albert shrugged. "We have done something. We've seen the theatre manager—he couldn't help. We've been inside the magician's dressing room—he wasn't there." He toyed, thoughtfully, with a tin of chicken-and-pilchard cat-food. "I can't think of anything else we *can* do," he said at last.

Emily Hollins picked up the handbag and folded umbrella she had just put down. "I can, Albert," she said. "Come on."

"But we've only just got back!" moaned Albert. "Where are we going this time?"

"Back to that theatre. We're going to do what we should have had the sense to do in the first place. We're going to take a good look inside that magic cabinet. *Come* along!"

The caravan door slammed shut behind them. The black-and-white stray cat miaowed noisily but unheard beneath the caravan floor.

The stage-doorkeeper, whose name was Edwin Harbottle, pursed his lips and frowned at the couple through the open window of his cubicle. "I'm not supposed to let any member of

the general public go backstage," he said.

Emily Hollins gripped her umbrella firmly. "We've already *been* backstage once," she said. "The manager took us. It's about our little boy, Henry. He went up on the stage this afternoon and vanished in your magician's cabinet."

The stage-doorkeeper chuckled through his straggly moustache. "That's what it's there for," he said. "Somebody goes inside and vanishes every time we have a performance."

"That may well be so," said Emily, haughtily. "But in the case of our Henry, he didn't come out again. It's my belief he's somewhere in your theatre still. Now then, are you going to let us go backstage and have a look for him—or shall I fetch the manager again?"

"Or," said Albert, pausing importantly, "shall we bring a policeman with a search warrant?"

"Oh, very well then—go on," said the stage-doorkeeper, realizing that he was beaten.

It was very dark on the stage. The curtain had been lowered and the lights turned out. Emily and Albert groped their way, nervously, to where they had last seen the magic cabinet. It was still there, standing in the wings between an acrobat's trampoline, a gold-painted plywood throne and half a dozen music stands.

"Now what?" whispered Albert.

"I'm going to have a really good look round inside it, of course."

"Do you think we should?" asked Albert, doubtfully. "I don't think it's allowed to mess about with magical things— supposing that magician comes back?"

"I'll give him a proper piece of my mind, if he does!" snapped Emily. "We wouldn't be here, would we, if he hadn't lost our Henry?"

Albert was forced to agree.

"You stand outside and keep an eye out," said Emily, "while I go in and have a scout around." With which, Emily opened the door of the magic cabinet and slipped inside. The door slammed shut behind her.

Albert Hollins waited for what seemed like several minutes, impatiently shifting his weight from one foot to the other and whistling, soundlessly, through his teeth. At last he opened the cabinet door no more than a couple of centimetres and called softly through the crack.

27

"Emily?"

There was no reply.

"Emily!"

Again there was no answer.

"Are you in there?"

Still nothing.

Albert Hollins stretched out a nervous hand and felt all round inside the cabinet. He could, he discovered, touch all four of the walls without actually venturing inside. He could not, he also discovered, touch Emily.

She was not inside.

The magic cabinet was empty.

"Well, I'm blowed," observed Albert, gloomily, to himself. "First Henry—and now Emily's disappeared as well!"

"I'm not putting these on!" gasped Henry, looking down in some dismay at the coarse woollen jerkin, the red hose and the roughly made shoes that Merlin had just handed to him.

They had gone back inside the cave and the magician had taken the garments out of a large cupboard.

"You can't go wandering around the countryside looking like that," said Merlin, pointing at Henry's everyday clothing.

"I don't want to go wandering around the countryside looking like anything," said Henry. "I want to get back to Cockleton-on-Sea as quickly as possible."

"All in good time, boy! First things first!" grumbled Merlin. "As I understood the matter, when we were in that theatre, you volunteered to be my assistant."

"No, I didn't!" objected Henry. "I didn't volunteer at all.

28

You shone a spotlight on me and Dad gave me a push. I didn't want to come up on to the stage. And if I'd known then that you were going to bring me back in time, hundreds and hundreds of years—I wouldn't have moved a centimetre from my seat. I only went up on to that stage to help with a conjuring trick."

Merlin wriggled his shoulders, huffily, and tugged at his beard. "I am Merlin, boy!" he snapped. "Magician at the Court of King Arthur—Grand Master in the art of all things appertaining to the mysterious and the magical—I will thank you not to refer to the wonders I perform as conjuring tricks." With which, and muttering under his breath, Merlin turned his back on Henry and resumed stirring the bubbling mixture in the cauldron.

"Sorry," said Henry.

Merlin did not reply.

Henry guessed that the old man was sulking. Very well, if the magician wasn't going to talk to him, then he wouldn't talk to the magician. Henry dug his hands in his trouser pockets and stared at the large toad which puffed its throat, croaked twice, and stared back at him, unblinking. The silence seemed endless. But if the magician wasn't going to speak to him, and he wasn't going to speak to the magician, that meant he'd *never* get home. Henry decided to pander to the old man's whim —for the time being, at least.

"How long do you want me to be your assistant for?" he asked.

Suddenly all smiles, Merlin peered over his shoulder. "Not long," he said. "Only until we have achieved the task that needs to be done."

"What task is that?"

The old magician pretended not to hear. He had ladled some of the messy grey-green goo into a small leather bottle. He held the bottle under Henry's nose. "How does that smell to you?" he asked.

Henry pulled a face. "Awful! It pongs like a mixture of bad drains and school-dinner cabbage."

"Excellent," said Merlin, slipping a stopper into the bottle and handing it to Henry. "Keep it about your person at all times and guard it well."

"What for?" asked Henry, turning the bottle over in his hands. "I thought you said it wasn't any good?"

"I said nothing of the kind, boy!" replied the cantankerous old fellow. "I said it wasn't any good for warts or festering boils. In which case surely, it follows that it must be good for something else! Kindly don't argue and keep your wits about you! And don't put it there!" he snapped as Henry moved to place the bottle in his trouser pocket. "Do as you've been told and put on the garments I gave you."

"Do I *have* to?"

"Yes. For your own good. If you were spotted walking about dressed up like that, you'd probably be mistaken for some evil sprite—or else a hobgoblin. Have you got any idea what they do around these parts with hobgoblins and evil sprites, if they should chance to get their hands on them?"

"I don't believe there's any such thing as evil sprites—*or* hobgoblins," said Henry.

Merlin sighed and shook his head. "You have a great deal yet to learn, lad," he said. "You'll be telling me next that you don't believe in fire-breathing dragons either?"

"I don't," said Henry. "I know that there were dinosaurs, of course—but they've been extinct for millions of years—long before man ever—"

Henry's words were broken off by the sound of a commotion outside which was growing louder every second.

First, there was a strident fanfare of trumpets, rising and falling on the afternoon breeze.

He could also hear the noise of horses' hoofbeats thundering across the grass. Coupled with this, there came the raised voices of men calling out, angrily:

"Have at thee, beast!"

"Take that, thou foul fiend!"

"A curse upon thee, evil monster!"

And there was another sound too: one which Henry did not recognize. It was a gasping, grunting, bellowing sound like that of some gigantic animal in fear and pain.

Merlin opened a small wooden window-shutter in the cave wall and beckoned for Henry to join him.

"Perhaps now you will believe in dragons," said the old magician.

Henry stared out of the window, blinked twice and swallowed, hard.

The fanfare had drifted across from the castle where a dozen or so heralds, wearing gaily coloured costumes and holding long, silver trumpets, were drawn up on the battlements.

The shouts and hoofbeats came from some half-dozen mounted knights, their lances dipped, urging their chargers across the countryside past the cave.

31

The gasping and grunting and bellowing was coming from an enormous dragon which was fleeing in terror, as fast as its old thumping legs would carry it, from the band of knights.

The dragon's barbed and scaly tail thrashed behind it, madly, in an effort to ward off the pursuers. Thick clouds of grey-black smoke belched out of the dragon's twitching nostrils and, every now and then, the frightened beast would turn its head and shoot back long tongues of orange-red flame and showers of sparks.

But nothing the dragon did, it seemed, could deter the fearless knights. Encouraged now by cries and cheers from a group of noblemen and ladies who had gathered on the castle's battlements to watch the sport, the band of mounted knights jabbed with their lances at the dragon's flanks and hacked with their swords at the unhappy beast's swishing tail.

"Die!" cried one of their number. "Perish, thou unspeakable devil!" He was the tallest of the knights: a thick-bearded man in golden armour sitting astride a snow-white mount and striking out at the dragon with a massive two-edged sword that flashed and gleamed as it swung in the air, catching the rays of the sun.

"That's King Arthur," sighed Merlin. "And that sword he's wielding is Excalibur. I'm afraid the poor dragon hasn't got a dog's chance."

Henry watched, sorry for the beast, as it raced off towards the horizon with the group of knights pounding at its heels, relentlessly sticking to their chosen quest.

"Are they really going to kill it?"

"I'm afraid so."

"Why? What has it done?"

The magician shrugged. "As far as they are concerned, boy, its very existence is its crime."

"That's not fair!" objected Henry.

"It is a dragon and they are Round Table Knights," said Merlin. "Besides, they'd hand out the same sort of treatment to anything they didn't comprehend. Sprites, for instance—or hobgoblins."

Henry Hollins, taking the hint, took off his trousers and T-shirt, and put on the coarse-woven jerkin and hose that the magician had given him.

3

The slight shower of rain had stopped as suddenly as it had started. All the same, it might just as easily begin again, and Emily Hollins chose not to take off her packaway see-through plastic raincoat. She removed her glasses, wiped away the few specks of rain that had been spoiling her vision, replaced the glasses on her nose and then peered again at the lowered drawbridge, raised portcullis, mighty battlements and turreted walls that were wondrous Camelot.

Emily was impressed, even though she was unaware that she was looking at the legendary home of King Arthur and his Knights of the Round Table.

"I suppose it must be somebody's stately home," she said to herself, and wondered who the owner might be.

A thought occurred to Emily. Feeling in her handbag, she took out the guide-book she had bought for fifty pence the day before in the Cockleton-on-Sea tourist office. The book contained descriptions of all the delights to be found in the little seaside town and its surrounding area. Emily flicked through the pages and quickly found the one she was seeking.

COCKLETON HALL is a small country manor house

situated some two miles north of the town going out past the boating lake and the bowling greens. The Hall is a fine example of fourteenth-century architecture, although some restoration work was carried out on the west wing in the latter part of the nineteenth century. Cockleton Hall is at present in the ownership of Colonel and Mrs C. J. Wentworth-Frobisher. Col. C. J. Wentworth-Frobisher (Retired) is willing to conduct visitors around the rose garden while the colonel's lady, Mrs Alice Wentworth-Frobisher, is renowned locally for her delicious cream-teas. Open to the general public between the hours of 2 p.m. and 5.30 p.m. on Tuesdays, Thursdays, Saturdays and Sundays during the holiday season.

Admission 30 pence
Children under twelve half-price
Dogs not allowed

"I'd hardly call that *small*," sniffed Emily to herself, gazing across at the tall towers with their fluttering pennants. "What a pity it's Wednesday," she added, wistfully. "I could just manage a nice cream-tea!"

Then, resolving that she would return to sample the delights the very next afternoon in company with Albert and Henry, Emily Hollins turned her back on the splendour that was Camelot and set off in the opposite direction where, she judged, Cockleton-on-Sea was situated.

Quickly dismissing the stately home from her mind, Emily Hollins set about collecting her thoughts. She had stumbled along the same dark tunnel and followed the same route as Henry had done over an hour before. She had taken the blackness of the tunnel in her stride, believing it to be no more than part of the magic cabinet's elaborate apparatus.

The cave, it must be admitted, had come as something of a surprise, particularly the bubbling cauldron and the croaking toad. Emily had expected that the tunnel would bring her out somewhere underneath the pier, and Merlin's strange dwelling-place had surprised her slightly.

But Emily Hollins was not the kind of woman who was easily deterred. She had set out with the intention of finding Henry, and she would go on looking until she *did* find him.

All she had found so far was Camelot.

Emily, assuming that Henry had walked through the cave in the same manner as herself, now also assumed that he too would be making his way along the footpath back to Cockleton-on-Sea.

She glanced up and down, but there was no sign of a *proper* road anywhere, let alone a bus-stop.

When she got back, she told herself, she would return to the theatre and give the manager a piece of her mind! And that conjuror too, if ever he turned up again. It was all very well inviting people up on to the stage to take part in magic tricks—but dumping them two miles north of the town with no means of getting back was quite another matter! And to do it to children too! Yes, she would certainly complain to someone.

Taking a firm grip on her handbag with one hand, and on her telescopic umbrella with the other, she trudged along the uneven path which led her to a little hump-backed foot-bridge.

It was here that Emily paused again.

For one thing, in a hollow beside the foot-bridge there were two of the sweetest, quaintest thatch-roofed cottages that she had ever seen. Hens scuttled in and out of the front door of one of the cottages while a goat chewed thoughtfully on some honeysuckle beneath the window of the second. But most surprising was the sight of a young woman apparently doing her weekly wash in the crystal-clear bubbling stream that ran under the bridge.

"Aw—poor thing!" said Emily to herself. "I suppose her washing-machine's conked out. I wonder she doesn't go to a launderette though—she won't get much of a lather in that cold water!"

There was something even stranger about the way the young woman was dressed. She was wearing clothes that were so old-fashioned they reminded Emily of an age long gone.

"I know what it is! She's either just come back from a Fancy Dress Parade or else she's going to one," Emily murmured under her breath, and then called out aloud: "I say—you, love—excuse me!"

The peasant woman, on her knees and concentrating on slapping her sodden washing against a large flat stone, had not noticed the newcomer on the foot-bridge. She glanced up now at the sound of the voice, and was more taken aback at the sight of Emily than Emily had been at the sight of her. The peasant woman had never seen a see-through plastic mac before—nor, indeed, had she seen *any* kind of plastic rainwear. Also, at the very moment that she chanced to glance up, the late afternoon breeze caught at the back of Emily's raincoat, whipping it out behind her like a transparent cloak.

The peasant woman, being a simple superstitious soul, sank

back on her heels, lost for words.

Emily, for her part, was not quite sure that she had gained the young woman's full attention and so called out to her again: "Good afternoon—I like your get-up." At the same time, she waved her folded telescopic umbrella.

Unfortunately, there was something wrong with Emily's umbrella. It had not been working properly for some weeks. The catch was broken. She had been meaning to get it mended but had not got round to it. The umbrella was inclined to fly open of its own accord and at the most inopportune of moments.

This was one of them.

The peasant woman watched, wide-eyed, as the strange black stick transformed itself, magically, into a large and sinister black mushroom-shaped object.

"Excuse me," Emily called across, "but could you point me in the right direction for Cockleton-on-Sea?"

The young woman did not appear to have heard. For some unknown reason she was shaking from head to foot. It also occurred to Emily that the young woman's eyes were fixed on the umbrella. So that was what it was!

"Silly me!" said Emily to herself. "The poor woman's worried about getting her washing dry. Because I've got my umbrella up, she thinks it's coming on to rain again!" She smiled at the young woman apologetically and called out to her, waving the umbrella, "Don't take any notice of my brolly! I'm afraid it's got a life of its own! It goes up by itself!"

But her words did nothing, it seemed, to calm the peasant woman's fears. Still on her knees and with one hand clutching her bundle of wet washing, she began to back away from the strange cloaked woman on the bridge who was waving the mysterious and enormous black mushroom at her.

"Don't go, dear!" Emily cried. "I only want to know which way it is to the town centre?"

"Witch . . ." muttered the peasant woman, still shuffling backwards on her hands and knees.

"That's right! Which way to Cockleton-on-Sea?"

The woman rose to her feet, slowly, the wet washing still held to her bosom. Stretching out her free arm she pointed a shaking finger at Emily. "Witch!" she cried again, then turned on her heels and fled towards the nearest cottage.

"It isn't going to rain—honestly—"

But the door of the cottage had already slammed behind the young woman and Emily was alone again.

"I'll just have to find my own way back," she told herself. Lowering her umbrella, she continued on her way, over the bridge and along the footpath.

It was a curious thing, but Emily could not rid herself of the feeling that several pairs of eyes were staring at her back from the cottage windows.

Henry Hollins half-hid himself behind Merlin's robes and tried to look as inconspicuous as possible.

They were standing by the huge fireplace in the royal bed-chamber where the atmosphere between the British monarch and his queen was a trifle icy.

"I do hope, Arthur, that you aren't intending to leave that dead dragon cluttering up the courtyard all night," Queen Guinevere said, glowering at her husband from the room's arched mullioned windows.

King Arthur muttered something under his breath and went on examining the blue-black bruise that ran the length of his shin.

"I can't understand," the queen continued, "why you will insist on bringing the bodies of the ugly brutes back to Camelot. It's not as if one could make a meal of them. You know as well as I do, dragon-meat is quite inedible. It tastes like a mixture of rotten herring and bad mutton."

"Ouch!" said King Arthur, having inadvertently touched a tender spot on the bruise.

"Arthur! Are you listening to me?"

"Yes, dear," said the king. "I'll get rid of the dragon's body first thing tomorrow morning. I brought it back because I want to have its head mounted and hung in the Great Hall."

"There are far too many mounted dragons' heads in the Great Hall as it is, Arthur! All staring down while you're trying to eat a meal. I don't understand why we can't have a nice tapestry on the wall like any other royal castle."

"And allow the great brutes to go rampaging around the countryside, ravaging everything in sight, I suppose?" said Arthur. He pointed at his wounded leg. "Look!" he snorted. "Just look what the ugly beast did to my leg!"

Guinevere sniffed. "It's no more than you deserve," she said. "If you will go hacking and cutting at dragons with that stupid great sword of yours, you can't complain if they attempt to get their own back occasionally—"

The queen broke off as she glanced out of the window again and saw a couple of serving-men in the courtyard trying to negotiate a carcass of beef around the sprawled hind-leg of the dead dragon which was blocking their path. In their turn, the serving-men were in the way of a couple of serfs who were dragging a wooden cart laden with two haunches of venison and the carcasses of several swans and peacocks.

Queen Guinevere frowned. "And who ordered all those groceries?" she said.

King Arthur coughed, nervously. "They're for the feast," he said.

"Feast? What feast?"

"Tonight's feast, my dear."

"You never said anything to me about a feast."

"I didn't think I'd need to. There's always a feast when we kill a dragon. I thought you knew that."

"That's absolute nonsense!" snapped Queen Guinevere. "You killed a dragon last week. There wasn't a feast then."

"No, dear," said King Arthur, choosing his words carefully. "That was because it was such a *small* dragon. It didn't seem worthwhile having much of a celebration. But the one we got today's a whopper, and so we thought—"

"We *can't* have a feast tonight, Arthur," wailed Guinevere. "I haven't got anything to wear!"

"I'm sure you'll find something, Gwinnie," said Arthur. He spread out his hands palm upwards, apologetically. "We can't cancel it now, my dear. Everything's been arranged. Serving-wenches, jugglers, tumblers, fools—"

"There is only one fool in this castle, as far as I am concerned," said the queen, coldly, "and he is standing not a thousand leagues from where I am at this very moment!" With which, she turned on her heel and stormed from the room, almost bowling over Henry Hollins in her haste.

King Arthur waited until the door had slammed shut behind Guinevere and then he glowered at his court magician. "Well, don't just stand there, Merlin," he snapped, jabbing a forefinger at his injured chin. "Attend to this!"

Merlin bowed low. "At once, your majesty," he said and turned to Henry who was still sheltering behind his back. "Hand me the magic ointment, boy."

Henry's startled face peered around Merlin's voluminous robes. "I haven't got any magic ointment," he whispered.

42

"I don't believe I have ever seen that boy before," said King Arthur, noticing Henry for the first time.

"He's my new assistant, your majesty," said Merlin, bowing low again and taking the opportunity to hiss at Henry: "Yes, you have! The stuff I gave you in the leather bottle!"

"Oh, *that* magic ointment!"

Henry fished the wart-and-festering-boil cure out of his jerkin. The old magician took the bottle from him and spread some of the contents over King Arthur's aching shin.

"How does that feel, majesty?"

The king waggled his foot and frowned. "About the same," he said.

"How did your majesty suffer the blow?"

"The ugly great brute swiped me with its tail," said Arthur, waving a hand in the air as he demonstrated how he got the wound, "at the very same moment that I plunged Excalibur into its side."

"With its *tail*?" Merlin sucked in his cheeks in worried fashion. "I wish you'd told me that before."

"Why?" snapped the king, suspiciously.

Merlin shrugged. "A wound caused by the *tail* of a dragon is the most difficult of all to cure."

"You mean your foul-smelling ointment isn't any good, I suppose? Exactly the same as that stuff you gave me for my wart last week." Arthur pointed to the small but offending growth on the third knuckle of his right hand. "That's still there," he said.

"I mean, your majesty," said Merlin, soothingly, "that a wound caused by a dragon's tail takes *time* to cure."

43

"It had better not take too long," said the king. "I shall require the use of both of my legs at the dancing after the feast tonight."

"By tonight, your majesty, the cure will have taken its effect—you will be fully recovered." Merlin bowed low yet again, and added: "You may have my word on that."

"Humph," grunted the king, unconvinced. He turned his gaze on Henry. "What's your name, boy?"

"H-H-H-Henry, your majesty," stuttered Henry. "Henry Hollins."

"That's a strange sort of name," frowned Arthur. "And which part of the kingdom do you hail from?"

"He is Henry *of* Hollins," Merlin put in, hastily.

"Hollins? Hollins?" muttered King Arthur. "I've never heard of the place."

"It's a tiny hamlet situated on one of the farthest borders of the farthest regions of your majesty's domain. The boy's father is Athelbert of Hollins—an apothecary. It was he that devised the recipe for the dragon's-wound ointment."

Merlin's words reminded Arthur of his sore shin. "It hasn't stopped hurting yet," he said, grimly.

"Not even a little bit?" asked Merlin.

"Not in any way whatsoever," growled King Arthur.

"It will, your majesty, before tonight's feast is over—in time for you to enjoy the dancing," and the old magician managed to raise a reassuring smile for the king.

"It had better," said the king. "For both your sakes. And now—begone. I don't want to set eyes on either of you again until tonight's festivities."

Merlin bowed low for the third time, then gestured to Henry, urgently, to get out of the room as quickly as possible.

King Arthur tested the weight of his sore leg on the flagstone floor.

"Ouch!" grumbled Britain's monarch.

Henry Hollins and Merlin the Magician were already on the other side of the thick oak door.

"Why did you tell him that my father's name was Athelbert and that he was an apothecary?"

Merlin shrugged. "I had to tell him something."

"You didn't have to tell him that my father invented your useless ointment," said Henry.

"It is not useless," objected Merlin, leading the way down the wide stone staircase. "That ointment will serve some extremely useful purpose—it's just that I haven't discovered yet what that purpose is."

"It isn't any good for warts or boils, you know that much," said Henry. "And, if you want my opinion, it isn't any good for black-and-blue bruises either."

"No," said Merlin, "I've got to agree with you on that point."

"And what's going to happen tonight, tell me that?" said Henry. "When your ointment hasn't done anything to make his leg better? What's *he* going to do to us?"

Merlin smiled. "But his leg will be better tonight," he said. "Once the king has had a flagon or two of wine and starts talking about old times with the Knights—he'll forget that there was ever anything wrong with his leg. He'll be dancing as well as anyone in Camelot." The magician took hold of Henry's

45

hand and looked down into his face. "Trust me," he said.

"I trusted *you* once before. When I stepped inside that magic cabinet. And look where that got me."

They had arrived at the foot of the stone staircase and Merlin, keeping a tight grip on Henry's hand, led him through a wide stone archway into the biggest, highest room the boy had ever seen.

"Gosh!" said Henry Hollins, gazing around and blinking hard.

Although it was still early evening, in the height of summer, only a little light could enter the castle through the small arched windows. The vast room was lit by dozens of rush candles which flickered in their holders, causing mysterious shadows to dance across the high vaulted ceiling. A fire glowed at one end of the room in an enormous fireplace where two serving-men were slowly turning a spit on which an ox was roasting. More serving-men were busying themselves about the room, laying out huge flasks of wine and wooden platters on a big, round table.

"This," said Merlin, pausing impressively, "is the Great Hall of Camelot."

But it was not the size of the room nor the activity inside it that had made Henry Hollins blink and gasp.

"Crikey!" he murmured, blinking for a second time.

All over the walls of the Great Hall were hung dozens and dozens of mounted dragons' heads. There were dragons' heads of all shapes and sizes. Some of them had forked tongues, some of them had long snouts. Some of them were bright green and scaly, some of them were dark grey and smooth. All of them

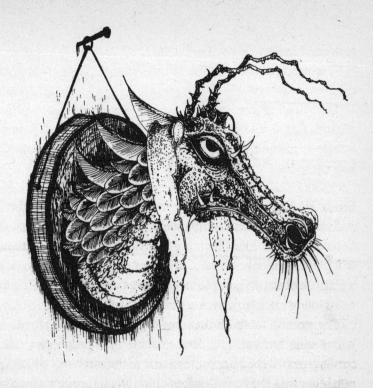

stared down solemn and unblinking. It seemed, thought
Henry, as if every one of them was looking straight into his
eyes.

"They're an endangered species now, you know," said
Merlin, sadly. "Someone's got to put a stop to it."

"Killing dragons?" asked the boy.

Merlin nodded. "Now do you see why I needed your
assistance? Do you understand now why I brought you back
through all the years?"

Henry did *not* understand. Not yet. But he did not tell the
magician so. He decided to wait and let Merlin explain everything to him in his own good time.

4

Emily Hollins took an even tighter grip on her black umbrella and shot a quick, nervous glance over her shoulder. It was, she decided, rather like playing at "Grandmother's Footsteps". Whenever she looked back, Emily never *quite* managed to catch a glimpse of anyone, but somehow she *knew* that several people were following her, dodging about behind the trees.

The uneven footpath that she had stumbled along for about half a mile had, at last, been crossed by a rough cart track. Emily had switched her route to that of the cart track which had taken her into the leafy bracken-thick wood through which she was now walking. The end of the wood was in sight, thank goodness. But Emily's heart sank as she realized that there was no sign of the town beyond the trees.

All that lay on the other side of the wood was more rolling countryside, stretching away as far as the horizon.

It was most peculiar, thought Emily. Why weren't there any *roads*? If she herself had lived in this area, she would have gone round to the District Council offices and complained most strongly. Good heavens, if people paid their rates, surely they were entitled to *some* services? It wasn't as if they were living in the Dark Ages!

Emily glanced back over her shoulder yet again and was surprised to discover that about a dozen people had come out of the trees and were ambling along behind her.

The more the merrier, thought Emily! At least they couldn't be muggers. Muggers didn't go about in gangs of twelve—or did they? Of course they didn't! They were most probably a party of hikers, Emily told herself. Or nature-ramblers, perhaps. In either case, they would most certainly know the area—they might even have a map.

She decided to wait by the side of the cart track until the group caught up with her. All her troubles would soon be over.

Except—the curious thing was that as soon as she stopped moving, all of them stopped too. They hung about in a bunch by the edge of the wood, peering across at where she stood.

This was getting more and more ridiculous!

And then a second group came out of the trees: about five or six of them, pushing some sort of cart. Emily watched as the two groups joined up with each other, and now all of them took a hand at pushing the cart. They began to move steadily towards her.

As they approached, she saw that the cart was a simple unpainted vehicle with solid wooden wheels. It had a kind of cage on top. The cage was roughly constructed like the cart, and had wooden bars. It was empty at the moment but looked big enough to take quite a large animal—a lion, say, or a gorilla, perhaps? But why should anyone go looking for a lion or a gorilla in Cockleton-on-Sea?

Good gracious! She hoped that some wild animal hadn't escaped from the small Safari-Park Zoo.

49

And now, as the group of people pushing and pulling at the cart drew even closer, another thought struck Emily. Every single one of them, she realized, was dressed in old-fashioned peasant-type clothing. And then she recognized one of them as the young woman she had come across doing her washing by the foot-bridge.

Of course! The Fancy Dress Parade! And the cart was going to be one of the floats in the procession.

Emily waved her closed umbrella at the oncoming cart-pushers and called out to them in cheery greeting: "Good evening, all!"

·The group pulled up short, with the cart, about twenty paces from where she stood.. Some of them exchanged nervous glances.

"Would you believe it—I'm still trying to find my way to Cockleton-on-Sea!" she said with a smile, addressing her words to the young woman she had recognized.

The young woman appeared uneasy at being addressed personally, and ducked out of sight around the back of the cart.

A heavily built man wearing a ragged jerkin and badly in need of a shave stepped forward. He seemed to be the group's spokesman. "Get in," he said, roughly, jerking a thumb at the cage on the cart.

"I'm not looking for a lift," said Emily in mild surprise. "Thanks all the same, but if you can point me in the right direction for the town centre, I'm more than happy to toddle along on my own."

"Get in!" repeated the unshaven one, in tones even brusquer than before.

"Really!" said Emily to herself. "Politeness doesn't cost anything—he might say 'Please'!"

On the other hand, she *had* walked for quite some distance and in new shoes which, she had realized, were a little bit too tight. Also, it was still extremely hot for walking, despite the fact that the afternoon had turned to evening. He *had* offered her a ride into town.

"Oh, go on then," said Emily, relenting. "Although I'm sure I'm going to feel a bit of a fool perched inside that thing!"

As she walked towards the cart, the unshaven man opened the cage. Emily pulled herself up and eased herself in through the barred door.

Emily was just a little perturbed when a sigh of relief went up from the Fancy Dress folk as she stepped inside the cage. She also thought it a little peculiar when the unshaven man slid home the bolt on the cage door. And why did he thrust his clenched fist in the air so triumphantly?

"I suppose it's just his little joke," Emily told herself. "I don't mind that—so long as they let me out of here before the Fancy Dress Procession begins!"

Then, chuckling to herself at the thought of being paraded along the promenade at Cockleton-on-Sea as part of a Grand Procession, Emily made herself as comfortable as possible inside the cage and waited for the journey to start.

To her surprise, instead of continuing along the cart track in the same direction, the Fancy Dress folk turned their vehicle around and set off again pushing it back towards the wood from which they had come.

"How funny!" mused Emily. "I must have been walking

away from Cockleton-on-Sea after all. But if the cart and the
group of Fancily Dressed people had been on their way to join
the Grand Parade—why have they chosen to turn back now?"

It was all very strange.

What was even stranger, though, was the way the Fancy
Dress folk were beginning to behave: taking it in turn to dance
around the cart, pulling faces at Emily and some of them, the
braver ones it seemed, poking their fingers through the bars at
her.

And what was the word they were whispering to one
another?

Emily listened carefully.

"Witch . . . Witch . . . Witch . . ."

"There are some funny people about," she said to herself. "I can't really complain though—after all, they are taking the trouble to push me back to Cockleton-on-Sea. It's all meant in good fun."

And she smiled, good-humouredly, and waved her umbrella at them through the bars of the cage.

The wooden cart-wheels creaked and groaned as they rolled over the ruts and hummocks of the uneven cart-track that led back towards Camelot.

Henry Hollins peered down over the turreted battlement at two snow-white swans swimming lazily between the lily-pond leaf clusters on the moat.

"What I don't understand," he said, "is why you had to pick on me—why couldn't you have chosen an assistant from your own time?"

Merlin frowned.

The old magician and the boy had come up on to the battlement, away from the noise and bustle of the preparations for the feast, in order to discuss the situation.

"A boy from this age would be absolutely useless," growled Merlin. "They're all brain-washed—they've been brought up to believe that dragons are a scourge and a pestilence to all mankind."

"And aren't they?" asked Henry. "Isn't it true then what King Arthur said? Don't dragons spend their time rampaging around the countryside, ravaging everything in sight?"

"Don't be ridiculous!" snapped the magician. "I chose you because you were intelligent, boy! Don't let me down. You saw the dragon hunt yesterday. Did that poor hunted half-crazed

53

beast appear to you as if it was capable of rampaging anywhere or ravaging anything?"

Henry thought for a moment and then shook his head. "No," he said. "I just felt sorry for it."

"There you are then," said Merlin.

"And are all the dragons as harmless as that one?" asked Henry.

Merlin nodded. "Every last one of them," he said.

Far below the old man and the boy, the white swans stepped out of the moat, stretched their necks, shook the water off their backs and preened themselves.

Merlin was lost in thought.

"Did you ever hear tell of the unicorn?" he said at last.

"Of course," said Henry. "They were like pure-white horses and they had one golden horn in the centre of their foreheads. But there aren't any left now, are there?"

"No, alas," said Merlin, sadly. "When the very last unicorn left this earth, the age of innocence was over. And when the last dragon is slain, then the age of chivalry will be dead."

The sun was just beginning to dip down over the rim of the horizon. A chill breeze whipped across the turreted battlement and Henry shivered slightly.

"How many dragons are there left now?" he asked.

Merlin shook his head. "Not many," he said.

"And how are you going to stop the dragon hunts? And what can I do to help?"

"I don't know," said Merlin, softly. "I don't know yet. We shall have to think of something."

The sound of raucous laughter rose from below. The

entertainers were just arriving and making their way across the drawbridge.

"It's time we went down and joined in the festivities," said Merlin.

The pier-master flicked a biscuit crumb from the lapel of his smart navy-blue gold-buttoned uniform blazer. He shook his head at Albert Hollins through the closed metal grille.

"I'm sorry," said the pier-master. "I'm afraid we're shut for the night."

"But I'm looking for my wife and son," said Albert. "They went inside a magic cabinet in the pier theatre this afternoon and neither of them came out again."

"Was it the cabinet that belonged to that old magician?" asked the pier-master.

"That's right," said Albert.

"Ah, I thought so. I went to see him last Monday night. I wasn't all that struck on him. I'd seen most of his tricks before. It's a pity you didn't go last week. There was a very good lady sword-swallower on instead of the magician. The Great Alma. She was very good indeed. She didn't only swallow swords, you know. She was a fire-eater as well!"

"I've heard about her," said Albert, a trifle impatiently. "She's not appearing this week because of a sore throat. But the whole point is, I'm worried about my wife and son. They've been gone for hours now. They vanished inside your theatre and I'd like to know what you intend to do about it?"

"It isn't *my* theatre," said the pier-master, huffily, straightening his shirt-cuffs. "You'd better come back in the

55

morning and see the theatre manager."

"I *have* seen the theatre manager. Twice. Once when Henry disappeared and then again after Emily went into that cabinet to look for him. Both times the manager told me to go back to the caravan and see if they'd turned up there." Albert Hollins turned and pointed towards the top of the cliffs where the caravan park was situated. "I've been up there and back again—*twice*! I'm shattered."

"It's a pity you didn't book your holidays for the month after next," said the pier-master. "We've got a new cable-car service opening up then. It'll get you from the promenade up on to the top of the cliffs for ten pence—or fifteen pence for the return trip."

Albert Hollins was beginning to lose his patience. "Where do I go to register a very strong complaint?" he said.

The pier-master took off his shiny peak cap with the gold-braided anchor and scratched his head. "Ah!" he said at last. "Now there you do pose a problem. It's a pity you can't leave it until next summer. We're opening an Information Office then, next to the kiddies' boating lake. That'll just suit your purpose."

Albert's patience snapped. "Look here, I'm not interested in what you're doing next summer," he said sharply. "Or in your cable car two months from now. Or even in your lady sword-swallower who was on last week, the Great Alma, or whatever she calls herself. It's here and now that I'm concerned about. I want to know what's happened to my wife and son. And if you can't help me, I'll find someone who can!" Mr Hollins turned his back on the pier-master and stomped off along the promenade.

"It's a pity you weren't here last year!" the pier-master called after him. "There was a gypsy fortune teller on the sands! I bet she could have been some use to you!"

But Albert was already out of earshot.

Some time later, Albert Hollins was sitting by himself at a corner table in the Harbour View Seafood Restaurant. He was considering his next move. On the table in front of him, untouched and already going cold, was a portion of crispy battered haddock, mushy peas and golden-brown chips.

"Try the peacocks' tongues, boy," said King Arthur, pushing a huge pewter platter of the delicacies across the Round Table. "They're stuffed with lark's breast and rosemary."

"No, thank you, your majesty," said Henry Hollins, partly because his mind was not on eating and partly because he was not used to such rich food.

"You ought to make a show of eating something, lad," Merlin whispered in Henry's ear. "He'll get suspicious if you don't."

Henry nodded and picked up between his fingers a piece of meat as large as any family Sunday joint off a tray of similar cuts. He made a pretence of nibbling at the joint but had already resolved that as soon as there was an opportunity, he would secretly slip the meat to one of the many large dogs that were padding around behind the diners.

King Arthur, however, had already dismissed Henry from his mind.

There was so much going on in the Great Hall.

A hundred more rush candles had been added to those previously lit and a warm, golden glow filled the vast chamber.

The head of the unfortunate dragon had already been removed from its body; mounted on a wooden shield it now hung in a prominent position among its fellows. The beast's sad, unseeing eyes gazed down upon the colourful scene below.

The jugglers were juggling.

The tumblers were tumbling.

The fools were making fools of themselves.

A whole host of serving-men and maids scurried to and fro between the fireplace and the table, fetching, carrying and replenishing platters as quickly as they were emptied.

The Knights and their ladies, seated around the Round Table, were gorging food and swigging wine as fast as it was put before them. They were all enjoying themselves enormously.

All, that is, with the exception of the queen.

"What I cannot understand, Arthur," said Guinevere coldly, "is why you got the carpenters to make this ridiculous piece of furniture in the first place!"

"Which piece of furniture is that, my dear?" replied Arthur, slurping at a golden goblet of rich, red wine.

"This stupid Round Table, of course!" snapped the queen.

King Arthur frowned. He glanced around. The Knights of Camelot had all stopped eating and were looking at their monarch, expecting him to stand up for the honour of the Round Table.

"It isn't stupid, my love," said Arthur, eyeing the queen nervously. "We chose the Round Table in order that no one should sit at our head—this way we are all equal."

"And I still say that it *is* stupid," replied Guinevere, tartly. "It's far too big for one thing—I can't reach anything that's in the middle."

"Is there something that I can pass you, your majesty?" said one of the Knights. He was a tall, slim young man with a gentle face and, as he spoke, he stretched out a hand towards a bowl of fruit in the very centre of the Round Table. "A peach, perhaps? My arms are longer than yours."

"That's Lancelot," whispered Merlin to Henry. "The noblest of all King Arthur's Knights."

"No, thank you, Lancelot," said Guinevere, coldly. "You only go to prove my point—how are we all equal when you can reach out and pick up things that I can't? If you want my opinion," she sniffed, tossed her head and turned back to

Arthur, "that makes us very *un*equal."

"Well . . . er . . . I don't know that . . . um . . ." muttered Arthur, shuffling unhappily on his throne.

The Round Table Knights and their ladies began to argue the matter between themselves, some of the shorter ladies taking Guinevere's side. Voices were raised, angrily, and tempers were on the point of being lost.

Happily, the argument was cut short as the Captain of the Castle Guard clomped into the room. He was a small man with a long sword which scraped along the flagstone floor, noisily, as he moved. A silence fell over the table as the Guard Captain crossed and whispered in the King's ear.

"What?" roared Arthur, sitting bolt upright on his throne and slamming the golden goblet hard down on the Round Table. "Have the hag brought in at once!"

"Yes, your majesty." The Guard Captain bowed low and scuttled from the Great Hall so fast that the tip of his sword threw up a shower of sparks as it scraped across the floor.

Arthur's eyes ranged round the Knights. "It seems," he said, a smile hovering on his lips, "that some of the peasants from the nearby village have succeeded in capturing a witch!"

"A witch?" There was an excited murmur from the occupants of the Round Table.

"What manner of witch, your majesty?" demanded one of the Knights, a beefy giant of a man whose name was Bedivere.

"An extremely fearsome one, by all accounts," said Arthur. "Even more terrifying than the one we caught last week—this one carries a magic mushroom and wears a coat-of-many-windows."

60

An apprehensive sigh ran round the room.

Henry, puzzled, glanced across at Merlin, who shrugged his shoulders.

It was at this moment that two enormous doors at one end of the chamber were flung open wide and a rough-hewn wooden cart creaked in, pushed by a number of villagers. Their spokesman, an unshaven fellow wearing a ragged jerkin, stepped forward.

"Your majesty," he cried, "behold the witch!"

As he spoke, the man threw out an arm towards a simple wooden cage that rested on top of the cart. Inside the cage sat a plumpish woman wearing a see-through plastic mac and clutching a folded black umbrella.

Emily Hollins beamed at the assembled company and waved her brolly, causing the faulty catch to dislodge again.

The black umbrella shot open with a jerk.

"Whoops-a-daisy!" said Emily.

The Knights of the Round Table drew back in alarm and some of their ladies hid their faces in their hands or ducked beneath the table.

"Gosh," gulped Henry. Then, turning to Merlin, he whispered: "That's my mum."

5

As soon as she realized that the Fancy Dress folk were pushing the cart towards the castle, Emily Hollins perked up with delight.

"Well, at least I shall get to see inside the stately home, even if I don't get one of their cream-teas," she told herself. "I suppose it's where the Fancy Dress Parade is starting from?"

Then, as the unoiled cart-wheels groaned and creaked over the drawbridge and under the portcullis, her eyes widened in wonder at the sight of the huge headless dragon in the courtyard, which she took to be some sort of float for the parade.

"My goodness me, that's lifelike!" she murmured. "It's amazing what can be done with some plastic sheeting and a few pots of paint!"

Next, as the large double-doors were opened, and she was wheeled into Camelot's Great Hall, Emily was further impressed by the feast spread out on the big round table.

There was roast goose; there was sucking pig; there was boar's head; there were all kinds of fruit; there was roasted haunch of venison; there were big boiled hams . . .

"If that's not better than a cream-tea," she told herself, "I don't know what is!" And she smiled at the people sitting round the table . . . more Fancily Dressed folk. And waved her umbrella at them. "Whoops-a-daisy!" she said out loud as the brolly flew open.

Her glance fell for a moment on a small boy who was sitting across the table and who reminded her a lot of Henry—except that he wasn't wearing Henry's clothes. And anyway, she asked herself as she refolded the brolly, what would Henry be doing in here? Just to make sure it wasn't him, though, she felt inside her handbag for her glasses. But before she could slip them on her nose, a voice addressed her, sternly.

"Stand up, witch!"

Emily peered across at the distinguished-looking gentleman who had spoken. He had a thick beard and wore a golden crown. The crown, she thought, looked very impressive, even though it was probably made of cardboard. She wondered if, by any chance, the man could be Colonel C. J. Wentworth-Frobisher (Retired), the owner of the stately home? In which case, the woman sitting next to him, also wearing a crown and looking at Emily down her nose, was probably Mrs Alice Wentworth-Frobisher of cream-tea fame.

"You heard his majesty, crone!" said the woman, though not too unkindly. "Get on your feet!"

Really! What did they mean by calling her names?

It occurred to Emily that the Fancy Dress Parade must have taken place earlier that afternoon and that the gathering she was attending was almost certainly a little party celebrating the event. No doubt the colonel and his lady had both had just one glass too many of the wine that was being passed around.

63

For one brief moment, Emily was on the point of giving them a piece of her mind. But no, she decided on reflection. After all, it was a holiday occasion. The country folk were enjoying some sort of medieval gala and who was she to spoil their fun? Besides, if she joined in the game, no doubt she'd be invited to join them at that groaning table and tuck into that mouth-watering spread.

"What's to be done with her?" said the man with the crown.

"Kill the hag!" cried a voice.

"Aye, kill the hag!" The call was taken up by more voices around the table. "Death to all witches!"

Henry turned to Merlin, horrified. "We've got to *do* something!" he urged.

"Ssshhh!" said the magician, placing a finger to his lips. "We can't interfere at the moment—we must bide our time."

"Take the witch down to the dungeons," said King Arthur. "We'll give her a fair trial later in the week and then she can perish at the stake along with that other witch we caught. We'll have a double burning."

The Knights of the Round Table thumped their goblets on the table, signifying their approval of their ruler's plan.

Henry chewed his lip nervously. It was all very well for Merlin to tell him not to worry, but what else could he do?

Emily herself was not so much worried at her predicament as downright annoyed. Instead of being invited to join in the feasting, she found herself being hauled away.

"And see to it that the magic talismans are taken from the crone!" called the king. "The coat-of-many-windows and the suddenly-appearing magic-mushroom. Without them the hag will be helpless."

"Just a minute!" Emily called back, rattling her closed umbrella against the bars of the cage. "A joke's a joke, but don't you think that this one's gone too—"

The rest of her words were lost as the cart was dragged out again through the large wooden doors which slammed shut behind it.

Merlin turned to Henry. "She'll have to spend the night in the dungeons, lad," he whispered. "We'll think of a plan for rescuing her tomorrow."

King Arthur looked across at Merlin sharply. "What's that about a plan?" he asked. "What have you got afoot for the morrow?"

"Nothing, majesty," replied Merlin, nervously. "No plans at all."

"Good! Excellent!" King Arthur paused to drain the contents of his fourth full goblet of rich, red wine. His cheeks were flushed and there was a sparkle in his eye. "Because I shall be requiring your services myself tomorrow, Master Merlin!"

"Mine, majesty?" quavered Merlin, his beard trembling nervously.

"Aye! If we are to combat evil, we shall need the help of as much magic as we can muster. We're setting out at dawn tomorrow on a quest!"

The Knights of the Round Table, who had also had more than their share of wine, cheered and stamped their feet. The ladies received the news more coolly and several of them frowned.

"What sort of a quest is it to be, Arthur?" demanded Bedivere. "Shall we seek out and slay another fearsome dragon?"

Queen Guinevere shot her husband a sharp glance. "Not *another* dead dragon," she groaned. "I sometimes think that Merlin has a point—what *will* you find to do when all the dragons in the land are slain?"

"Go after all the one-eyed ogres!" cried a Knight.

"Destroy all two-headed giants!" called another.

"But what quest are we embarking on tomorrow?" repeated Bedivere.

"Why don't we seek the Holy Grail again?" suggested Lancelot, the noblest of the Knights.

"Frankly, I'm beginning to tire of the Quest For the Holy Grail," said Arthur, stroking his beard. "If you want my opinion, it's starting to look like a waste of time." He paused, looked all around the room, and thought hard. There was total silence from the Round Table as the Knights waited, eagerly, for the king to continue. "Why don't we," he said at last, "allow adventure to take care of itself and tackle any evil adversary that dares to cross our path?"

The Knights of the Round Table cheered again at this and toasted the proposition with more red wine.

It was at this point that the dungeon-keeper entered. He was a short thick-set man with bulging biceps. His dark eyes peered out from a black skull-cap mask which came down over his ears and nose. He brought in with him two objects which he placed in front of Arthur. One of these was Emily's folded see-through plastic raincoat. The other was her closed umbrella.

Arthur got to his feet, unsteadily, picked up the brolly and the plastic mac and held them high above his head.

"These magic talismans will serve to make us invincible to all evil forces!" he cried. "Whosoever chooses to defy us—be it foul-winged beast or evil sprite—shall be cut down!"

The Knights of the Round Table lumbered to their feet and applauded their monarch loud and long.

Queen Guinevere took advantage of all the noise to whisper to her husband, "Only remember what I said, Arthur—no more dragons!" Her eyes ranged round the many sad-eyed dragons' heads mounted on the walls. "I sometimes think we women could manage things *so* much better than you men! Hanging tapestries would look *much* nicer."

"How long will you be gone?" murmured Henry to the magician anxiously.

Merlin shook his head. "Who knows? When Arthur and the Round Table Knights set out on one of their adventures, there is no such thing as time."

"But *about* how long?" persisted Henry.

"It may be a day or it may be a week—or it may be a year."

"A whole *year*!" gasped Henry.

"At least with Arthur and his Knights away, you'll have a chance to get your mother out of the dungeon," whispered the magician.

"*How?*"

"You'll think of something, I'm sure," replied Merlin, unconvincingly.

"I can't think what. And even if I did, I couldn't begin to get us back to Cockleton-on-Sea without your help."

"Don't worry. I may not be away all that long."

But Henry *was* worried.

★　★　★

It was some time before Emily Hollins accustomed her eyes to the dungeon's darkness. It had already taken her some time to get over the rudeness of the black-masked man who had snatched the brolly out of her hand and also taken the raincoat off her back. It had taken more time too to get over being pushed down a long winding flight of stone steps, manhandled along a damp, rush-lit passage and then thrust, roughly, through the door of her present chill quarters.

Looking back over everything that had happened to her that afternoon and early evening, Emily Hollins was slowly coming to the opinion that there was more to her present situation than she had previously thought. These curious events, she now decided, must have been caused by more than just a common-or-garden Fancy Dress Parade or a simple Country Gala.

She would need to sit down, quietly, and think things out.

There was just enough light filtering into the dungeon through the peephole in the door for Emily to make out the flagstone straw-strewn floor for a couple of metres in front of her. But it was impossible for her to tell the size of her prison, or even to guess at what horrors, dangers or creepy-crawly things might lie in the darkness beyond her vision.

Still, first things first, she thought, plumping up sufficient of the straw to make herself more comfortable. Then, settling herself on the makeshift seat, Emily gave her mind to considering her situation . . .

"Excuse me, love?"

The voice that broke in on Emily's thoughts came out of the darkness across the dungeon. The fact that she was not alone came as a shock to Emily and she jumped with surprise.

68

"I'm sorry if I startled you," said the voice, "but do you
think you could oblige me with the right time?"

Straining her eyes and peering into the dark, Emily made out
the figure of a young woman sitting opposite her on the floor.
Emily peered at the wrist-watch with the luminous face which
had been a birthday present from Albert only a year before.
How far away was Albert now! "It's twenty past eight," she
said.

"No, you don't understand my meaning," said the young
woman.

She got up and came over to Emily. She was a pretty young

woman with curly golden hair and, Emily was delighted to see, she wasn't got up in Fancy Dress. Or was she? For although she certainly wasn't wearing an historical costume, like everyone else that Emily had come across, the young woman wasn't exactly dressed in *ordinary* clothing either. She had on a short flouncy frock covered all over in red and gold sequins.

"I don't mean what *time* is it," said the young woman. "I mean what *Time* is it?"

Emily, flummoxed, glanced at her watch again. "Well," she began, "I may be five minutes fast, but—"

The young woman shook her head and her golden hair bounced on her bare shoulders. "I mean what *Time* is it historically speaking? What Age are we in?"

Emily hesitated. "Well—sort of *now*, isn't it?"

"But *is* it?" persisted the young woman.

"It was when I got up this morning," said Emily, doubtfully, "because there's a calendar in the caravan and I remember glancing at it most particularly, and . . ." Her voice trailed away. So much had happened since she had got out of bed that the morning seemed like a thousand years away. More, perhaps . . . "What Age do *you* think it is?" she asked.

The young woman shook her head, not answering the question. "Did you, by any chance, happen to go inside a big black box in the pier theatre at Cockleton-on-Sea?"

Emily nodded, excitedly. She had something in common with the young woman. Emily had almost forgotten the magic cabinet which, she suddenly realized, must have had something to do with her present predicament.

"We're both in the same boat then," said the young woman.

"Allow me to introduce myself. I'm the Great Alma."

"Wait a minute!" The name had struck a chord in Emily's memory. "I remember! You're the sword-swallower who was appearing at the theatre last week!"

The Great Alma nodded. "I do fire-eating too," she said.

"You should have been on this week as well," said Emily, "only you've got a sore throat?"

The Great Alma gave a rueful smile. "I did have a bit of a sore throat," she said. "But I wouldn't let that stop me performing. No way. I've always got a sore throat of some kind. All sword-swallowers suffer from sore throats."

"I can well imagine," said Emily sympathetically.

"My goodness me," said the Great Alma, "if I let a little thing like a sore throat keep me off the stage, I'd never ever give a performance!"

"What happened to you then?" asked Emily, patting the pile of straw that she had heaped into a cushion. "Why don't you sit down here, beside me, and tell me all about it?"

The Great Alma sighed. "There's not a great deal to tell," she said, accepting Emily's invitation and joining her on the straw. "It was after Saturday night's performance. I was sitting in my dressing room. Everyone else had gone home. I'd just taken two teaspoonfuls of throat medicine when I suddenly remembered that I'd left one of my swords at the back of the stage. I went to look for it—it was quite dark, not a soul about—and, lo and behold, there's this funny big black box standing up in a corner. I'm afraid I've always been a bit of a busybody. I couldn't resist a peep inside. But as soon as I was in the door slammed shut behind me. I couldn't get out again.

71

The next thing I know is I'm walking down this long dark tunnel—"

"Say no more," Emily broke in. "I know the rest of the story."

"It's my opinion that it's some sort of Time Tunnel," said the Great Alma.

"Well, I never!" gasped Emily.

The Great Alma nodded, firmly. "I think we've been transported back through history."

"Whatever will they think of next!" said Emily in some astonishment.

The Great Alma frowned. "But tell me about you," she said. "How did you come to get inside the magic box?"

Emily explained about the magician and how she had set out in search of Henry.

"Then your little boy's come back in time as well?" said the Great Alma. "Poor little mite! He must be wondering what on earth has happened!"

"I'm sure he is," said Emily.

"It must be very worrying for you."

"It is. Although to tell you the truth," said Emily, perking up a little, "I will say this: he's usually very good at taking care of himself."

"That's something to be grateful for."

"Now that I come to think of it," said Emily, thoughtfully, "I did notice a little boy who looked very much like Henry at a banquet that was going on upstairs. I didn't give much thought to it at the time, because it seemed so unlikely, but what with all these other strange things going on . . ."

Emily broke off as a flap opened in the bottom of the door and two wooden plates containing food were pushed into the dungeon.

The Great Alma picked up one of the plates, glanced at the contents ruefully, and handed it to Emily. "Let's hope it *was* your little boy that you saw," she said, "because if he *is* at a banquet, he's certainly much better off than we are."

"Good gracious me!" said Emily, wrinkling her nose up at the food. "What on earth is this mess supposed to be?"

"Scraps and leftovers," said the Great Alma sadly.

"Is this all we get?" asked Emily, shocked.

"That's it," said the Great Alma. "It's all I've had to eat for days."

"Cheer up!" said Emily. "Worse things happen at sea. Besides, the more I think about it, the more I'm coming to the opinion that it *was* our Henry I saw upstairs. And if he saw me, which I'm sure he did, he isn't going to let the grass grow under his feet. He'll think of something."

"I only hope you're right," said the Great Alma. "Because if he doesn't help us to escape from here, I don't know of anybody else who might."

"I'm sure he will." Emily smiled, encouragingly, and then glanced at her watch. "Mind you, it's getting close to his bed-time now, so I think we'll probably have to wait until tomorrow. The best thing we can do is try and get some rest ourselves. If we *are* going to escape from here, we're going to need all our strength." She snuggled down in the straw. "I don't think I'll have much trouble dropping off, in spite of everything—it's been quite an eventful day."

73

But the Great Alma showed no sign of getting ready for sleep. Having swallowed the last few morsels from her platter, she was now gazing enviously at Emily's untouched food.

"Aren't you going to eat your supper first?" said the Great Alma, wistfully.

Emily pulled a face. "I never was a great one for leftovers."

"I hope you won't think me a proper greedy-guts," said the Great Alma, "but would you mind if I had yours—rather than let it go to waste?"

"Of course not, dear. Be my guest."

The Great Alma tucked into the contents of the second platter hungrily. "It's just that it's been so long since I had a real sit-down meal."

"Waste not, want not," said Emily. "In any case, I'm trying to lose a bit of weight. Besides, I had an *enormous* lunch at that café opposite the pier before we went to the show this afternoon."

"I know the one!" said the Great Alma, excitedly. "It's got fishing nets and plastic lobsters hanging on the wall! What did you have?"

"Well now, let me see . . . Roast pork; crackling; stuffing; creamed potatoes; choice of two vegetables and jam roly-poly and custard to follow—" Emily broke off as she noticed a tear creeping out of the corner of the Great Alma's eye. She could have bitten her tongue off at her lack of tact. "Don't cry, dear," she said, softly. "Henry's sure to get us out of here. Things will look much brighter in the morning, just you wait and see . . ."

6

The fretful clatter of horses' hooves on cobblestones broke the silence of early morning. A cock crowed in the distance and an old black crow preened its wings on a parapet. The two white swans from the castle moat waddled into the castle courtyard in search of kitchen scraps for breakfast. A grizzled sentry on a watchtower yawned and scratched himself under his armpit.

King Arthur tugged impatiently at the reins of his charger and counted the men on horseback for the umpteenth time. Himself included, there were only four: the others were Lancelot, Bedivere and Merlin. The two Round Table Knights, like their monarch, were sitting astride richly caparisoned steeds. The magician was perched on an old warhorse, called Cerebus, brought out of retirement for the occasion.

The gallant old charger had been enjoying its hard-earned rest and resented being pressed into service. It had already made two unsuccessful attempts to unseat Merlin who had the uneasy feeling there were more to come.

The first rays of sunlight crept over the turreted walls down into the courtyard where they gleamed on the Knights' burnished armour.

King Arthur was not wearing armour, apart from his plumed helmet. Instead, he had on Emily's see-through plastic raincoat. He had tried putting on his armour earlier that morning but had soon realized that the mystical coat-of-many-windows would not fit over the top. He had decided that the coat-of-many-windows would provide him with much more protection than mere tailored metal.

He had the added benefit of the powers of the magic mushroom. The faulty catch had worked its mischief again that morning and the umbrella had flown open the moment that Arthur took hold of it. He was sitting under its shade now. He felt that it would ward off any evil spirits.

The king frowned as he gazed out from under the umbrella at his two Knights and his court magician. "Are you *sure* there are no more of my Round Table abroad this morning, Merlin?" he said.

"Positive, your majesty," replied the magician, struggling to keep his seat as the old warhorse kicked out its hind legs yet again.

Arthur sucked in his cheeks morosely. It was very dis-appointing. He had expected a much bigger turn-out than this.

On the previous night, in the warm glow of the Great Hall fire and with their spirits boosted by comradeship and rich red wine, the entire body of Round Table Knights had sworn unswerving allegiance to him. They had loyally declared their intention of accompanying him on the quest—no matter into what dangers he might lead them.

But in the chill grey light of early morning, the prospect of rumbustious adventure did not seem half so enticing. Some of the Round Table Knights had shivered and snuggled back under the sheepskin bedclothes pretending not to have heard the first cock-crow; while others had lain abed moaning and groaning, feigning illness.

It was all extremely unsatisfactory so far as Arthur was concerned. "Well, then? What are we waiting for?" he grumbled at his companions impatiently.

"Ready and willing at your command, my liege!" said Lancelot, the sunlight twinkling on his armour.

"Yours to command until death, sire!" said Bedivere, gripping his lance.

"And what about you, Merlin?" said Arthur, suspiciously, glancing across at the old magician who was gazing about him, open-mouthed. "What are you sitting there catching flies for?"

"I'm just waiting for my assistant, majesty," said Merlin. He had not set eyes on Henry that morning and was wondering what might have happened to the boy. "I sent him off to fetch a magic potion for your majesty's protection. I feel it would be foolhardy to set out on a perilous journey without it."

"It's not that smelly green stuff you've been rubbing all over me for weeks, I hope?" said Arthur, irritably. "The rancid muck that's supposed to cure everything from warts and boils to bruises?"

Merlin twitched, nervously, but did not reply.

"We've got all the charms we need already, man!" snapped Arthur, waving Emily's brolly in the air and bracing his shoulders in her see-through raincoat. "And why is the youth taking so long about bringing this magic potion?"

"I've no idea, majesty," said Merlin, preparing to slip out of

77

the saddle. "I'll go and . . . Oooh-*ERR!*"

Merlin's cry of surprise was caused by Cerebus who, taking advantage of the old man's attention being directed elsewhere, had reared up suddenly on its hind legs. The trick had worked. Merlin grabbed at thin air and landed on his behind, with a jolt, on the cobblestones.

"Ouch," said Merlin, testily. "That hurt!"

"Get up, you old goat," snarled King Arthur.

"I think I may have done myself an injury," replied the magician, rubbing gingerly at his backside.

"Good, I'm glad to hear it!" There was more than a hint of malice in King Arthur's voice. "You can rub some of that stinking green stuff on it—it's about time you had a taste of your own medicine."

Sir Bedivere sniggered.

King Arthur glanced around. "Where *is* that boy?" he said, and then called out at the top of his voice: "Boy! *BOY!*"

Arthur's cry echoed round the courtyard causing the old crow on the parapet to flap its wings and fly away with a complaining "Caw!"

Henry Hollins, hiding in the shadows at the bottom of the winding stone steps that led down to the castle dungeons, chewed at his lower lip. He could hear King Arthur calling him.

The boy had slipped away, before first light while the castle was still asleep, in the hope of managing a word with his mother through the dungeon door. But he had arrived at the bottom of the dungeon steps only to discover that he was not the only person awake at that hour. On peering cautiously around the corner, Henry had spied the black-masked dungeon-keeper sitting wide awake and motionless at the end of the rush-lit passage, keeping an all-night watch over his prisoners.

For over an hour, it seemed to Henry, the dungeon-keeper had not moved a muscle. And now, just when the man had yawned and let his head sink on to his chest, King Arthur's voice echoed down the winding staircase.

"Boy! *BOY!*"

And the dungeon-keeper had heard it too, for his head jerked up and he shook himself awake again.

"Where are you, boy? Show yourself!" bellowed Arthur from above.

Henry heaved a sigh. There was no way now that he would be able to sneak a few words with his mother. Sadly, he turned and set off up the worn stone steps.

"What were you doing down there, lad?" snapped Arthur as Henry stepped out from the darkness into the blinding daylight.

"I . . . I lost my way," said Henry, blinking as the morning sunlight streamed on to his face.

Merlin, he saw, was sitting on the cobblestones and looking miserable while Arthur, Lancelot and Bedivere circled around him on their horses. Henry hurried across and helped the old magician to his feet.

"What happened?" asked the boy.

"The ugly brute threw me," said Merlin, wincing as he tried to move his aching joints.

"Nonsense!" said Arthur. "The old fool fell off his horse. It appears that he's in no condition to accompany us on the quest.

You'll have to come instead."

"B-b-b-but . . ." began Henry.

"But me no 'buts', boy!" The king spoke sharply. "Get up on that steed. If I'm not to take a magician, at least I'll have his assistant with me."

"'You'd better do what he says, lad," muttered Merlin, in pain, it seemed, from head to foot.

"What about Mum?" whispered Henry, urgently. "If I go with King Arthur, you must promise me you'll get her out of that dungeon the minute we leave."

"I will! I will! Only, *please*, do as he says or he'll begin to suspect that we're planning something."

"What are you two whispering about?" demanded Arthur, adding weight to Merlin's words.

"Nothing, majesty," said the magician, with a low bow. "I was just advising the lad on how to handle the horse."

"If he takes your advice on that subject," growled Arthur, "he'll end up on his backside like yourself!"

Sir Bedivere guffawed and even the noble Lancelot found it hard not to smile.

Henry clambered up on to Cerebus's wide back.

There was a swish as Arthur tugged the jewelled Excalibur from its scabbard. He waved the sword three times above his head and the broad blade caught the sunlight.

"To chivalry and adventure!" cried the monarch, urging his mount forward.

"To chivalry and adventure!" echoed Bedivere and Lancelot. Their chargers' hooves clattered across the courtyard cobblestones as they set out in Arthur's wake.

"Gee-up!" said Henry.

Cerebus shook his head, snorted, and held his ground.

The old warhorse, which had a mind of its own, thought things over for several seconds. If it *was* going to be pressed back into service, it would certainly be more pleasant to gallop around the countryside with this boy on its back rather than suffer the weight of a full-grown man . . .

"Gee-up!" said Henry again.

Oh, very well then. The warhorse took the bit between its teeth and set off at a sudden canter in pursuit of the three horses that had gone before.

Henry was almost unseated by the unexpected movement but he managed to hang on. He managed, too, to turn his head and call back at the solitary figure standing in the courtyard.

"You won't forget, will you, Merlin?"

"I won't!"

And then Cerebus and his rider swept out under the portcullis gate leaving the old magician alone in the courtyard.

Merlin rubbed at his bruised behind. All at once, his shoulders drooped and he let out a long sigh. He didn't feel very well. He was far too old, he told himself, to go tumbling off a horse on to cobblestones. His old bones ached abysmally. He was only surprised that he hadn't done himself a more permanent injury. It wouldn't have been so bad if the cobblestones had been dry, but they were still soaked with dew.

"*AtishooOO!*"

He had almost certainly caught a cold. He was also far too old to be wandering around at such an early hour. What he needed, most of all, was a hot drink and a long lie-down. He limped out of the courtyard and set off in the direction of the cave.

The old magician frowned as he limped along. Something was bothering him. He was getting so long in the tooth, he told himself, that his memory was beginning to fail. What was it that the boy had asked him not to forget? He couldn't for the life of him remember. Oh well, it was probably nothing very important . . .

Down in the dank dark depths of the castle dungeon, Emily Hollins had heard the drumming of the horses' hooves as they crossed the drawbridge.

Emily wondered what was happening.

The Great Alma, sleeping like a baby, had her head nestled in Emily's lap. But Emily, finding sleep impossible, had been awake all night reflecting on her situation.

Her immediate prospects, she was forced to admit, did not seem all that bright. Her one hope lay in Henry. But could she be absolutely sure that it *had* been Henry she had seen sitting at the feast? And, even if it *was* him, could she also be absolutely sure he had recognized his mother through the bars of that cage? And, even if it *had* been him and even if he *had* spotted her predicament, could she then be absolutely sure he would be able to come to her rescue?

She had spoken reassuringly enough the night before to her young companion who was sleeping so soundly now. But, in her heart of hearts, Emily was not half so confident as she had tried to sound.

And just supposing that Henry was now a prisoner somewhere in the castle like herself? She was his mother, after all. Surely it was her job to go to *his* aid, rather than sit here moping and hoping that he might come to hers?

The thing that finally galvanized Emily into action was a rustling sound in the straw in the darkest corner of the dungeon. Probably a mouse, she told herself. The possibility did not alarm her, for mice held little fear for Emily Hollins. But just supposing it was . . . a *rat?* Emily gulped and shuddered. Rats were an entirely different kettle of rodent altogether.

Arriving at a decision, she shook the Great Alma gently.

"Wake up, dear!"

The Great Alma blinked and opened her eyes.

"What is it? What's happened?"

"Nothing—yet," said Emily, reassuringly. "But I don't think we ought to rely on Henry getting us out of this pickle. We ought to tackle the job ourselves."

The Great Alma frowned. "That's easier said than done," she said. "That door's shut fast. I've been in here since last Saturday night and it hasn't been opened once."

Emily clambered to her feet and glanced out cautiously through the barred peephole in the door. The black-masked dungeon-keeper was sitting across the passage scratching himself, thoughtfully, with his right hand under his left armpit.

"If we can't open the door ourselves," said Emily, turning back to the Great Alma, "we'll have to find a way of getting Cheerful Charlie out there to do it for us."

"But *how?*"

Emily considered the problem for several moments and then she opened her bulging handbag. "Considering everyone seemed so taken with my plastic mac and that old brolly," she

said, "perhaps there just *might* be something in here that will take his fancy." And Emily burrowed in the contents of the handbag.

Out in the rush-lit passage, the dungeon-keeper had switched hand and armpit and was now scratching, thoughtfully, underneath his right arm with his left hand.

"Excuse me, but have you got a minute?" Emily's smiling face appeared at the peephole.

The dungeon-keeper, whose name was Ulric the Oppressor, glanced up at Emily and scowled. "There isn't any food," he said, now scratching with both of his hands at his enormous stomach. "There'll be no more kitchen scraps for you prisoners until the dogs have finished with them."

"I don't want any food," said Emily, "thank you very much."

Ulric the Oppressor blinked and frowned. This was the first prisoner he'd ever had in his charge who didn't want food. "Oh?" he said. "What *do* you want then?"

Emily's smile widened. "I don't want anything at all, thanks all the same."

"Then why are you bothering me?"

"I want to show you something."

"If this is some sort of trick . . .?"

"It isn't a trick. Come and look."

Ulric the Oppressor pulled himself to his feet and crossed to the door of the dungeon.

"There," said Emily.

Ulric looked where Emily was pointing across the dungeon. His mouth dropped open and his eyes widened in surprise. A strange bright light was dancing mysteriously in the darkest corner of the dungeon. Ulric the Oppressor licked at his dry lips. It was the most wonderful thing that the dungeon-keeper had ever seen in all his life. Not that he had witnessed much that was wonderful in his lifetime.

Truth to tell, Ulric the Oppressor was almost as much a prisoner underground as any of his charges. He was on duty twenty-four hours a day and worked a seven-day week. The times when he was allowed out of the dungeon area and up into the daylight and the sweet fresh air were few and far between. So few, in fact, that he could only bring to mind the one occasion . . .

It had happened many years ago. It had been on the day that

Arthur assumed the throne: a public holiday. Ulric had been no more than a youth at the time and employed as an apprentice dungeon-keeper to his father, Claud the Cruel. Man and boy, they had come up out of the dungeons into the castle courtyard. Ulric could still remember the blue sky and the white clouds and how warm the sun had been on his face. There had been dancing lights on that occasion: the sun's rays prancing about amongst the water-lily leaves on the moat and dancing too between the rustling green-and-golden leaves on the trees. It had been the happiest day in Ulric the Oppressor's life . . .

There was a sad, wistful look in the dungeon-keeper's eyes as he gazed through the bars of the peephole at the dancing light.

"What is it?" asked Ulric, softly.

"I don't know," said Emily.

Emily was not telling the truth. The light came from the tiny key-ring torch that had been at the bottom of Emily's handbag. It was dancing now because the Great Alma was waving it about in the furthest, darkest corner of the dungeon. Emily had hoped that the light might prove attractive to the dungeon-keeper but she had had no idea how much it would mean to him.

"I want it," stated Ulric the Oppressor.

"Come in and take it," said Emily. "It's yours."

The light had stopped moving. This was because the Great Alma had placed the torch on a ledge and then rejoined Emily by the door of the cell.

Ulric the Oppressor slipped back the bolt on the door and entered the dungeon. The pin-point beam of light appeared to hang in mid-air, tantalizingly still, inviting him to stride across and snatch it out of the darkness.

"Can I keep it?" he asked.

"I don't see why not—if you can catch it," replied Emily. "But if I were you, I wouldn't rush at it. You might easily frighten it away."

Ulric the Oppressor nodded. There was, it seemed to him, sound sense in the witch's warning. He set off, on tiptoe and ever so slowly, across the stone-flagged floor. As the dungeon-keeper reached out a shaking hand and took hold of the light, Emily and the Great Alma slipped out through the open door. They hurried along the rush-lit passage and set off up the worn stone steps that led to freedom.

The dungeon-keeper did not even notice that they had gone. He was squatting on his haunches on the dungeon-floor, crooning softly and holding the small bright light in one hand as he stroked it with the other.

And then disaster struck.

As the dungeon-keeper stroked the key-ring torch, his fingers inadvertently moved the tiny control-button. Ulric the Oppressor had no idea what he had done. He only knew that the light had gone—that what he had just acquired had disappeared—as far as he knew, for all time.

The dungeon-keeper's head sank on to his chest. His shoulders heaved. A strange strangled murmur came from his lips. For the very first time in his life, Ulric the Oppressor was crying.

7

"Tallyho! There he goes, men! After him!" cried King Arthur, waving Emily's open brolly above his head, the see-through plastic raincoat ballooning out at his back. He took a tight rein on his charger and then eased it forward down the steep gully after his quarry. The horse's hooves slipped and slithered on the loose stones sending them cascading on ahead.

"Yoicks!" called Sir Bedivere, tilting his lance and forcing his own steed to follow close on Arthur's heels.

"The beast's making for that forest!" cried Sir Lancelot, unsheathing his sword and galloping hard along the brow of the gully. "I'll try and cut it off!"

"I don't know what they're making such a fuss about," sighed Henry to himself, perched on Cerebus's broad back and trailing some two hundred metres behind the other three riders. "It's a very *small* dragon."

But the actual size of the dragon was of little importance to King Arthur or either of his two Round Table companions. At that moment, any dragon was better than no dragon at all.

They had ridden all day, never stopping for food or drink, with not so much as a glimpse of a two-headed giant or a one-eyed ogre to show for it. The old warhorse, Cerebus, had long

88

since tired of trying to match strides with the younger, fitter horses and, despite all Henry's entreaties, had dropped further and further behind.

Then, as the afternoon shadows lengthened into those of evening, the two knights and their sovereign dismounted, having decided to seek shelter for the night. It was at this point that the woodcutter had appeared and told them of the dragon that was roaming the district. By the time that Henry had caught up with them, the three had re-mounted and were setting off in search of the dragon. Cerebus fell into step with the other horses and the four of them jogged along in line.

"I thought you told the queen that you weren't going to kill any dragons on this adventure, your majesty?" Henry said to the king.

"Nothing of the kind," Arthur replied. "I promised Guinevere that I wouldn't take any more dragons' *heads* back for the walls."

"What will you do with this one if you catch it then?"

Arthur shrugged. "Kill it first and think about that question later," he growled.

"I have heard tell," Bedivere put in, "of one noble who uses the heads of the dragons he vanquishes as footstools."

"What a good idea!" Arthur enthused, but on second thoughts he frowned. "But I don't think that Guinevere would stand for that one. She moans loudly enough about the dragons' heads on the walls—I can't imagine what she'd be like if I suggested dotting them around the floor as well."

"We could impale this one on Camelot's topmost turret, my liege," said Lancelot, "as a warning to all other foul beasts not to invade your territories."

"We could do that, we could indeed do that," Arthur agreed. Then, turning to Henry, he continued: "There are a hundred and one things you can do with a dead dragon, for instance—"

But Henry was not to learn the other things for which a slaughtered dragon could be put to use. It was at this point that their quarry had been sighted.

The chase was on.

Henry had been right. It *was* a small dragon. Little more than a dragon-cub, in fact, and hardly as big as Arthur's horse.

But the dragon's size was to prove more of a help than a hindrance to the creature in the hunt that followed. The young dragon was far more agile and cunning than the lumbering full-grown versions of the species. It twisted and turned and ducked and dodged and then doubled back on its own trail, leading its pursuers on a wild-goose chase through the most unpleasant areas of the countryside. And only occasionally did they even so much as catch a glimpse of the speeding creature.

"A plague upon thee, evil fiend!" cursed Sir Bedivere, as his horse floundered in soggy marshland.

"Have at thee, vile beast!" cried the bold Sir Lancelot, as the dragon led him through a particularly thorny thicket.

"Hold still, accursed creature, and let me at thee!" grunted King Arthur, as he pursued the young dragon through a thick plantation of pine trees where the sharp pine-needles scratched at his face and hands and even, to his consternation, tore at the coat-of-many-windows.

Puffing and panting, and with their mounts bowed down

under the combined weight of armour, arms and rider, King Arthur and his accompanying knights struggled ever onward without once really coming to grips with the nimble-footed dragon.

"Wait for me!" called Henry, as he and the aged Cerebus were very soon left behind again. "Just a minute! *Please!* Do wait for me . . ."

And when, eventually, the boy and his horse did catch up with the other three, it was very nearly dark. Arthur, Bedivere and Lancelot had dismounted and just about recovered their breath as they talked in whispers at the edge of a bramble thicket.

"What's happening now?" asked Henry, lowering himself thankfully from Cerebus's broad, uncomfortable back on to the solid ground below.

"Ssshhh!" whispered Lancelot, putting a warning finger to his lips.

"We've got the evil brute pinned down in there," muttered Sir Bedivere, nodding at the dense bramble thicket.

"That pine wood the accursed creature led me through must have been bewitched," said Arthur with a scowl. He held up, for Henry's benefit, the plastic see-through raincoat which was covered with tiny rips and tears. "Methinks they were not pine-needles I encountered, but a thousand thousand demons from Hades that had taken on the form of pine-needles. What do you think, boy?"

"Dunno," said Henry, non-committally. In fact, he knew quite well what he thought but had no intention of being drawn into an argument with the monarch.

"Then you *ought* to know!" Arthur's voice rose, angrily. "You're an apprentice-magician, aren't you? It's your business to know such things. If you can't tell the difference, lad, between a pine-needle and a demon from Hades, you'll not make much of a magician!"

That's as maybe, thought Henry, *but if you don't know the difference between a magic cloak and a plastic see-through raincoat, you're not so bright yourself!* But aloud, he said: "I'm sorry, your majesty."

"Ssshhh!" whispered Lancelot again, peering into the gathering gloom of the thicket. "I thought I heard something moving in there."

All four of them listened carefully. Lancelot was right. There was a sound coming from the very heart of the bramble thicket. A sort of sniffling, snuffling, shifting sound.

"If you ask me," said Sir Bedivere, "the ugly brute is settling down for the night."

Arthur glanced up at the swiftly darkening sky. The moon was not yet up but two early stars were glowing brightly overhead.

"It's getting too dark to flush the creature out," said Arthur. "I suggest we think about some sleep ourselves. We'll light a fire, cook some food, and then get some rest."

"What if the beast attempts to escape under the cover of darkness?" asked Lancelot.

"I doubt that it will," said Arthur. "Dragons are not nocturnal beasts. We'll take it in turn to stand vigil, though, just in case. We'll draw lots to see who stands guard first. Tomorrow morning, as soon as the sun is up, we'll cut our way into the thicket, and . . ." Arthur left the sentence unfinished, but his right hand went to the jewelled hilt of Excalibur and his meaning was plain.

Henry Hollins shuddered.

"You can make yourself useful, boy," said Arthur, catching Henry's eye. "Forage around and fetch some firewood."

"Yes, your majesty."

Henry set off, skirting the edge of the thicket, picking up such wood as he could find. But his mind was not really on the task. He wondered about his mother and whether Merlin had been able to help her. He wondered too about the dragon. Occasionally his glance strayed into the bramble bushes. There was no sign of the creature. Neither was there any sound now. But he knew it was in there . . . somewhere. Lying low, afraid to come out, scarce daring to breathe and with its heart pumping fast inside its scaly body.

It wasn't fair, thought Henry. Three grown men to one small dragon. And it was not as if the poor creature had done anything to harm anyone. What was it that Merlin had said? When the last dragon was slain, then the age of chivalry would be dead . . .

"Boy? Boy!" King Arthur's voice drifted across at Henry on the late evening breeze. "Where are you, boy?"

Henry glanced back the way that he had come and saw a rosy glow which told him that they had already lit the fire. He could hear Bedivere's bellowing laughter. Better make haste, he told himself, and get back with the firewood he had collected. Gathering his bundle together and clutching it tight with both arms to his chest, Henry set off in a stumbling run towards the

93

warm glow of the fire.

One thing at least was certain. If he could think of a way in which he might help the dragon to escape before the night was over, he would not hesitate to do so.

The moon was out, bathing the towering walls of Camelot in a grey and ghostly light. A sentry, high up on a turreted battlement, paused to glance down at the silver surface of the moat and then resumed his patrol.

"There's a big black bank of cloud coming up," whispered Emily Hollins, taking a firm grip on her handbag and peering cautiously out of the hiding-place she was sharing with the Great Alma. "As soon as the moon's behind it," she continued, "we'll make a run for those trees."

Emily and her companion had remained hidden in the same place since early morning.

Their escape had been discovered almost immediately. The shouts of Ulric the Oppressor had brought men running to the dungeon from all directions. And then, from morning until dusk, armed search-parties had scurried in and out of the castle, their footsteps echoing urgently under the portcullis gate and clattering across the wooden drawbridge. There had been so many comings and goings in and out of the castle that the drawbridge had not been raised all day.

Which was extremely fortunate so far as Emily and the Great Alma were concerned. For it was underneath that very draw-bridge that they were hidden. Only once had they been disturbed. That was when the two white swans had waddled under the drawbridge, stretched their long necks, examined the two intruders closely, flapped their wings in disapproval and then, fortunately, turned and waddled off again.

But all day long, Emily and the Great Alma had not dared to speak and scarcely moved a muscle for fear of being discovered.

Now, with the oncoming of night, the passing to-and-fro across the drawbridge had ceased and the castle seemed asleep.

The Great Alma broke the silence. "I aren't half hungry," she whispered despondently, and added: "*and* cold."

Things had been bad enough before in the damp dark dungeon, but here there was a chill breeze cutting underneath the drawbridge and her short sequin-spangled fire-eater's costume offered little or no protection against the cold. The Great Alma shivered. Her teeth chattered and she rubbed her upper arms with her hands.

"Cheer up, Great Alma," said Emily. "At least we're free." She rummaged in the contents of her handbag and produced a half-empty packet of sweets. "Here, suck one of these Exceedingly Strong Peppermints. It might not do much for your appetite, but it might help to warm you up a bit."

"Ta, very much," said the Great Alma, gratefully popping a peppermint into her mouth.

The full moon slipped behind the black bank of cloud which had crossed the sky.

"Now's our chance," whispered Emily. "Come on!"

Then, with the Great Alma close on her heels, Emily stole out of the shadows beneath the drawbridge and sprinted, as fast as her legs would carry her, down the wide green sloping meadowland that lay between the castle and the shelter of the fringe of trees ahead.

It seemed a long, long way across. Emily's heart was beating pitter-pat, both with the exertion of running hard and at the fear of being discovered in headlong flight. To make matters worse, the moon slid out from behind the cloud before they reached the safety of the trees. The Great Alma's sequinned costume was suddenly bathed in silver light.

Up on the battlements, the sentry blinked as he caught a glimpse of a distant scurrying figure whose upper half appeared to be covered in myriad twinkling lights. The sentry rubbed his eyes and looked again. But whatever it was that he thought he had seen—either flashing demon or glittering sprite—the apparition had disappeared as quickly as it had showed itself.

The Great Alma flung herself down beside Emily in the deep bracken underneath the trees and lay there for several seconds, panting furiously.

"Are you all right, Great Alma?" asked Emily, anxiously.

"I . . . I think so," gulped the Great Alma, rolling over onto her back and fanning at her open mouth with her hand. "But my goodness me," she gasped, "these peppermints of yours—aren't they *strong*?"

"They're meant to be strong," replied Emily with a chuckle. "But I wouldn't have expected peppermints to have that much effect on a fire-eater and sword-swallower!"

An owl hooted overhead and a small black furry creature broke from cover close by and scuttled past them on the way to its lair.

Emily and the Great Alma got to their feet hastily and brushed themselves down.

They examined their surroundings. Moonlight streamed

through the lattice-work of branches over their heads and they could make out a footpath, close at hand, leading away from the castle, through the trees, and on towards a seemingly impassable cliff-face beyond.

"Well?" asked the Great Alma. "What's next on the agenda?"

"The first thing I've got to do is find our Henry," said Emily.

The Great Alma glanced back the way they had come, at the black and uninviting outline of the castle silhouetted against the night sky. "Supposing he's still in there?" she said.

Emily bit her lip. "I don't think he is," she said, shaking her head. "I'm sure he'd have got word to me somehow if he was."

"But if he *isn't* there, where is he?"

Emily sighed. "Your guess is as good as mine," she said.

"Then how do you propose to set about finding him? Where do you begin to look?"

"All I can do is ask," said Emily, but her words belied her anxiety. "I've got a tongue in my head if nothing else."

"Ask where?" persisted the Great Alma. "Ask *who*?"

"Everybody and anybody," replied Emily with determination. She nodded back the way they had come. "Beginning with him," she added.

The Great Alma, surprised, followed Emily's glance. A solitary cloaked and hooded figure was walking along the path in their direction. It was still some distance away and would not have been visible but for the glowing lantern swinging from one of its hands. Plainly, the figure was not aware of Emily and the Great Alma who were still standing in the shelter of the trees.

"Supposing it's someone who's been sent to look for us?"

said the Great Alma. "Supposing he raises the alarm?"

"That's a risk I shall have to take," said Emily, firmly. "But there's no reason why you should take it too. You can stay hidden in the trees and let him think I'm on my own."

"Not likely!" The Great Alma tossed her golden curls. "We've come this far together, Mrs Hollins . . ." She paused, and then continued: "Is it all right if I call you Emily?"

"Of course. Please do—all my other friends do."

"Well then, we've come this far together, Emily—we might as well see it through together to the end."

Emily smiled at the Great Alma gratefully. Then, when the hooded figure had almost drawn level with them, they stepped out from their hiding-place together.

"Excuse me," said Emily, "but you wouldn't happen to know anything about a boy called Henry Hollins, I don't suppose?"

The hooded figure stopped short in surprise and then held up the lantern to Emily's face. "Yes, I do," said the figure. "I know you, too. You're his mother, aren't you? I've just been to the castle to look for you."

Emily peered back into the face still half-hidden by the cowl, but the lantern's glow was sufficient for her to realize that she had seen the man before. "I know you, too," she announced. "You're that magician who got our Henry up on the stage. It's because of you he arrived here in the first place."

The old man nodded. "My name is Merlin, magician at the Court of Arthur." He paused and then turned his lantern towards the Great Alma. "But who are you?" he said.

"She's the Great Alma, sword-swallower and fire-eater from

the South Pier Theatre, Cockleton-on-Sea," said Emily. "It's all your fault she's here as well—and me. I think you've got some explaining to do, Mr Merlin."

The old magician nodded, slowly. "I suppose you're right," he said, a trifle sadly. "Come with me."

8

Smoke drifted lazily from the deep-red glowing embers and spiralled up towards the night sky. Henry Hollins threw on another log, disturbing the camp-fire which spat and crackled angrily, throwing upwards a shower of golden sparks. The noise caused one of the nearby tethered horses to whinny and Sir Bedivere's regular snores were interrupted for a moment as he started in his sleep. Then, as orange flames leapt up from the log that Henry had added to the fire, Sir Bedivere settled back into his rhythmical snoring and all else was silence.

They had dined, frugally, on nuts and apples and berries which Arthur had produced from a pack he carried. This somewhat meagre repast had been supplemented by some little cakes that Lancelot had concocted out of flour, oatmeal and clear spring water, then baked on hot flat stones at the edge of the fire. It had been a simple meal and yet one that Henry Hollins had enjoyed hugely, eaten under a canopy of twinkling stars and in the company of King Arthur and the two Round Table Knights.

Afterwards, they had drawn lots for guard duty. Lancelot had drawn first sentry-go; Bedivere had stood the second; and now it had fallen to Henry's lot to keep watch and feed the fire until the velvet sky turned into rosy dawn. Arthur, because he was the king, was not expected to stand guard.

Henry folded his arms around his shins, settled his chin on his knees and gazed into the heart of the fire. Then, despite the glowing heat, he shivered involuntarily as he was suddenly consumed with a deep feeling of loneliness. He glanced across at the three sleeping figures but their presence did not dispel his sense of isolation. Next, the boy's eyes strayed to the neat stacks of burnished armour which the men had removed before settling down to sleep. Beside one of these gleaming piles were two unlikely objects: a telescopic brolly and a rather tattered folded see-through plastic raincoat.

The sight of these familiar articles reminded Henry of his mother and caused a lump to rise in his throat. But Henry Hollins was not a boy who gave way easily to emotion. If he was going to be of any use at all, not only to his mother but also to himself, he would need to keep his spirits up and his wits about him. This was no way at all to behave, he told himself. Angrily he blinked back a tear and swallowed hard.

He was even more annoyed at himself then, as he became aware of the sob that had sounded at the back of his throat. But the anger turned to surprise as the sob was followed by another—louder this time—and he realized that it was someone else who was doing the sobbing. The sounds were coming from deep inside the thicket. Not only that, but they were growing noisier with every second and were already threatening to drown out Bedivere's snores.

Henry clambered to his feet softly and tiptoed across to the edge of the thorn bushes. He tried to part them and peer inside but the thorns were too sharp and the branches too tightly interwoven.

As well as the young dragon's sobbing, Henry could also hear again the creature's quick and urgent panting. There could be no doubt that, as the night-hours slowly passed, the dragon had lain awake and its terror had increased while its fear of the oncoming dawn had grown and grown and grown . . .

The boy glanced at the soundly slumbering men and the anger in him rose once more. How could they be so totally uncaring? How could they talk of chivalry and honour and, in the same breath almost, conspire to kill a harmless creature that couldn't even protect itself?

"Don't be afraid," he whispered into the thorn bushes. "I'm coming to get you out of there. I'm going to help you to esca—" He broke off at a sound behind him.

But he turned to find that it was only the blazing log falling into the fire. Reassured, but with his own heart beating faster, Henry set off around the perimeter of the bramble thicket, looking for a gap through which he might enter the bushes.

Arthur and Lancelot slept on, soundlessly, while Bedivere's thick black moustache trembled with his snores.

It did not take Henry long to discover the place where the dragon itself had entered the thicket. The branches were broken and the undergrowth trampled down, leaving a sort of dark prickly tunnel more than large enough for the boy to go inside. Carefully, mindful of the needle-sharp thorns that jutted out at him from every angle, he edged his way deeper into the thicket. The closer he got to the dragon, the louder grew the creature's panting and then, as he turned a sharp brambly corner, Henry felt its hot breath on his cheek.

Henry stopped short and stared hard into the darkness ahead. Then, as his eyes focused on the tight lacework of branches, he became aware of a pair of large round startled eyes staring back at him. The boy stood stock-still, seeing that the creature was trembling slightly.

"It's all right," he murmured, softly. "Don't be afraid. I've come to help you."

Slowly, he stretched out a hand towards the scaly head which had not taken its eyes off him for a single second. The dragon was silent and quite motionless except for an occasional shiver. But as Henry's outstretched fingers came close to the long, thin snout, the dragon twitched in momentary fear. Henry watched as a grey-green wisp of smoke curled out of each of the creature's gaping nostrils.

"Easy . . . Easy there . . ." said Henry, softly.

And then, still murmuring reassuringly, he stretched his hand out again and this time the dragon remained still and allowed his finger-tips to stroke its snout which felt tough and leathery to his touch.

"Good boy!" he said, and: "Who's a good beast, then? Who's a clever dragon?"

Bit by bit, he felt sure that he was gaining the dragon's confidence. Not only was it now allowing him to stroke it, but it also seemed to be nuzzling against his hand. He moved another step towards it and the dragon let him pat it firmly along its long broad neck.

"Come on, old lad," urged Henry, attempting to coax the nervous creature out of its hiding-place. "Come with Henry."

Again it seemed as if the dragon moved a shade closer to him. Oh well, thought Henry, here goes then! And, summoning all of his courage, he took a firm hold on a handful of the loose skin under the dragon's pointed ears and gave a gentle tug.

"Come on then, Draggie," he said, softly but encouragingly. "Let's get out of here."

The dragon, placing one hesitant three-webbed foot after the other, allowed the boy to lead it out of the bramble-thicket.

Henry paused and gazed across the moonlit countryside. There was rolling meadowland as far as the eye could see in every direction. Which way should he go? Henry shrugged. It didn't really seem to matter where they went so long as he and the dragon put as much distance as possible between King Arthur's party and themselves before the sun came up.

"We'd better be on our way then, Draggie," said Henry, still keeping a guiding hand on the creature's leathery neck. "Walkies!"

And boy and beast set out together across the moonlit grassland. They had not been walking long before Henry began to get the odd feeling that it was not himself guiding the dragon, but the dragon taking him where it wanted to go.

Emily Hollins stared at the huge speckled toad which was blinking at her from a corner of the cave. The toad croaked twice as Emily placed her spoon in her empty bowl and set it down on the floor beside her.

"Have some more soup," said Merlin.

"No, thank you," said Emily. "It was *very* nice, though," she added politely. "Very nice indeed."

"Mmmmm!" agreed the Great Alma, licking her own spoon enthusiastically. "Scrummy!"

"If you're sure you've had enough, then?" said the magician. He lifted the soup-pan off the fire and replaced it with the cauldron of green gooey-stuff that he didn't quite know what to do with.

"Getting back to the subject of our Henry," said Emily, returning to the thought that was uppermost in her mind, "I still think you took too much upon yourself—bringing him back in Time the way you did. You might at least have asked permission first from myself or Mr Hollins."

"I'm very sorry," said Merlin. "But I was in need of an assistant rather urgently. And I would have kept an eye on the lad and returned him safely when I'd finished with him."

"Kept an eye on him?" scoffed Emily. "I don't know how you've got the cheek to say that when you don't even know where he is at this particular moment!" She paused and nodded at the Great Alma. "And what about this poor young lady? Look at what she's had to put up with—being locked up in that dirty dungeon for days. All that was because of you."

"I didn't know anything about that," said Merlin, giving the Great Alma an apologetic smile. "I was in Cockleton-on-Sea when all that happened."

"It was still your fault, though, wasn't it?" persisted Emily. "It was you that left the magic cabinet lying around in the theatre."

"I didn't imagine that anyone would go inside it without being asked."

"What nonsense!" said Emily. "I went inside it myself. It

was sheer downright carelessness on your part." She glanced across at the darkest recesses of the cave where the Time Tunnel began. "For all we know, there might be someone stepping inside it right this minute. We don't know who might appear next: that stage-doorkeeper; the theatre manager, perhaps; or even the ice-cream lady."

Merlin shook his head. "I've learned my lesson on that score," he said. "I've closed the tunnel."

Emily sniffed. "That's what I call shutting the stable-door after the horse has bolted," she said. "And how do you propose that we all get back again?"

"I'll open it whenever you wish," said Merlin. He turned to the Great Alma. "You can go back this minute if you're ready."

"No, thanks." The Great Alma shook her golden curls. "I've already told Emily that I'd stick it out with her to the bitter end. I wouldn't dream of going back before her little boy is safe and sound."

"Which takes us back to where we were before," said Emily. "You got us into this mess, Mr Merlin—it's up to you to get us out of it. How can we find Henry? Where do we begin to look?"

Merlin, who was stirring the messy green liquid gently in the cauldron, paused as an idea suddenly struck him.

"I wonder . . ." he murmured, "I wonder if . . ."

"If what?" asked Emily, impatiently.

Merlin pointed at the cauldron with his ladle. "This stuff in here. I wonder if I gazed into it, and concentrated hard, whether I might be able to see what's happening in any place in the world?"

"Is that what it's for?" asked Emily, doubtfully. "Is that

what you're supposed to do?"

"That's just my problem," sighed Merlin. "I don't *know* what it's supposed to do. I know what it *doesn't* do. It doesn't cure warts or festering boils. And it doesn't do much for dragon-bruises either."

"It smells *awful*," said the Great Alma, wrinkling her nose as she peered into the cauldron over Emily's shoulder.

"Doesn't it just!" agreed the old magician. "That proves it must be good for something. I'll *try* peering into it and concentrating hard—you never know, it might just work."

Emily and the Great Alma held their breath as Merlin stared into the bubbling green goo, muttered several magical incantations under his breath and waved his long fingers over the cauldron mysteriously.

107

"Well?" said Emily, unable to contain herself any longer. "What can you see?"

"Nothing," said Merlin, sighing again. "Nothing at all except bubbling green stuff."

"Steady, Draggie! Slow down, boy!" Henry panted, tightening his hold on the dragon's neck as it quickened its pace yet again and its tail swung to and fro, excitedly.

The boy and the dragon were speeding through a tangled wood where thick green bracken grew waist-high and the morning sun twinkled down on them through a patchwork of leafy branches. Judging by the sun's position in the sky, Henry guessed that they must have been on the move for about five hours. By now, he guessed, they had put miles and miles between themselves and King Arthur's party. In all the time they had been on the move, they had paused only once to quench their thirst at an ice-cold crystal-clear spring they had come across, bubbling out of a rocky bed.

Henry was more than ready for another stop, but the dragon had other ideas. There was no doubt at all now in the boy's mind that the creature knew *exactly* where it was heading for. Not only that, but Henry also sensed they were not far from that destination. Ever since they had entered the wood, the dragon had been sniffling excitedly, twitching its snout and letting out small puffs of grey-green smoke from its nostrils.

"Whoa! Take it easy!" groaned Henry, as the dragon suddenly took it into its head to change direction. Dragging the boy along with it, the creature veered off through a clump of bluebells and then down a slippery steep-sided mossy bank.

Henry struggled to stay on his feet as the dragon slithered down to the bottom. Then, without pause, the creature plunged on through an ankle-deep rushing woodland stream and up the opposite bank.

Determined not to lose his hold on the dragon, Henry clung tight grimly and matched the creature stride for stride as it careered through more bluebell patches and clumps of bracken towards a patch of daylight that marked the edge of the wood.

Then, as they broke from cover and entered a clearing bathed in morning sunlight, the dragon came to a sudden halt. Henry, loosing his hold on the creature's neck, flung himself thankfully down on the ground and gulped at air. He lay quite still for several moments on his back, staring up into the blue sky.

Gradually, as his own panting diminished, he became aware of other noises close at hand: gruntings and snufflings and the sounds of huge feet padding across the clearing. Henry rolled over on to his stomach and raised himself up on to his elbows. The sight that met his eyes caused him to blink with surprise.

Across the clearing was a rock-face with an enormous cleft in it that marked the entrance to some sort of quarry. And out of that quarry, lumbering towards him, was an entire family of dragons of all shapes and sizes and numbering about ten in all.

As Henry watched, the young dragon waddled across and nuzzled up to one of the larger of the approaching beasts, rubbing its snout along the bigger one's scaly hide. The large dragon, which Henry took to be the mother, stuck out a long,

pink tongue and gently licked at the young dragon's soft under-belly while a couple of tiny dragons gambolled playfully around.

Henry surmised that the young dragon, *his* dragon, had found its way home.

One by one, the members of the dragon family turned and ambled back towards the shelter of the quarry. The biggest dragon of them all, a massive, proud silvery-green specimen, brought up the rear, flicking out a forked tongue and turning its head this way and that for signs of danger. Then, one by one again, the dragons padded out of sight into the quarry until only Henry's dragon and the largest one remained.

The young dragon turned, looked back at Henry through round soft eyes, wagged its tail at him in friendly fashion and then followed its fellows. The biggest dragon also took a last look at Henry, swivelling horny head on leathery neck and peering across at the boy who was still sprawled out on his elbows in the grass. And then, as if saying "thank you" for the safe return of the young dragon, the giant dragon lifted its snout and let out a long low crooning bellow. Two tongues of orange-red flame whipped out at its nostrils and stabbed at the sky. And then the last one of the family of dragons turned and went the way of the others, into the quarry.

Henry, alone in the clearing, clambered to his feet. The air was still. Not so much as a blade of grass stirred. A single cricket was chirruping somewhere but there was neither sight nor sound nor smell of a dragon. It was almost as if the boy's meeting with the dragon family had never happened.

The quarry was a fantastic hiding-place, thought Henry. The dragons would be safe enough from dragon-hunters in there. Now that this little adventure is over, he said to himself, my next problem is how to get back to Camelot and do something about Mum before —

"Well done, lad!" It was King Arthur's voice that interrupted Henry's thoughts. He spun round and gazed across at the three motionless figures sitting astride their chargers in the shadow of the trees.

For one brief moment it occurred to Henry that the three men might have only just arrived and therefore not seen the dragons, but his wild hope was quickly dispelled.

"Well done indeed, boy!" said Sir Bedivere. "You've led us straight to the lair of the last pack of dragons believed to be ravaging Britain."

"They aren't ravaging anywhere!" replied Henry stoutly. He shivered, in spite of the fact that he was standing out in the sun. "What are you going to do?" he asked anxiously. It was a pointless question for he already knew the answer.

"I'll tell you what we're *not* going to do," said Lancelot. "We're not going to let the pack of them get away like the first one did."

King Arthur chuckled and turned in his saddle. "Ride as hard as you can to Camelot, Lancelot," he said. "Summon all the Round Table Knights and bring them here as quickly as you can. Tell them there's going to be the biggest dragon-hunt in history."

"Yes, my liege," said Lancelot, and straightaway he urged his horse back through the woods the way they had come.

As Arthur and Bedivere dismounted, Henry strode across the clearing and confronted the king. "Merlin says that when the last dragon is slain, the age of chivalry will be dead."

"Merlin's a silly old fool," said Arthur.

Bedivere had unsheathed his sword and was testing its keenness on his thumb. "I'll need to find a stone to sharpen this on," he said. Then, glancing across towards the quarry, he continued: "Are you sure there isn't another way out of there?"

"Positive," said Arthur, shaking his head. "I've been in these parts before. I know that quarry well. That's the only exit there is. And the rock-face inside is high and steep on all sides. Fear not, Bedivere—the evil brutes are at our mercy."

"Supposing they try to run for it before Lancelot and the Round Table Knights arrive?"

Arthur shrugged. "The opening's so narrow they could only

come out one at a time. Between the two of us, Bedivere, we could cut down quite a few of them as they come out. The rest we'd soon round up and slay when Lancelot gets back." King Arthur paused and smiled at the downcast Henry. "Cheer up, boy!" he said. "You look as if you'd lost a gold-piece and found a groat!"

Henry chewed at his lower lip and did not reply. But underneath his breath he muttered to himself, "It's all my fault . . . I led them here . . . It's all my fault . . . It's all my fault . . ."

9

Henry Hollins watched anxiously as the Knights of the Round Table adjusted their armour, attended to their horses' trappings and, worst of all, honed away at their sword-blades and lance-tips.

Almost an hour had passed since Lancelot had returned, at full gallop, with the entire band of King Arthur's men in full array. Since their arrival, the Knights had busied themselves with preparations for the slaughter that lay ahead. Nothing, it seemed, could save the dragons. Sir Bedivere, who had been on guard at the entrance to the quarry from the moment that Lancelot had set out to bring the reinforcements, now gave a broad sweep with one arm to signal that the dragons were still safely assembled in the quarry, unaware of the fate that lay in store. Then, having given the signal, Bedivere set off across the clearing to where his own horse stood tethered.

"Mount!" called the king.

All along the fringe of the wood, the Knights of the Round Table swung themselves up into their saddles and took a firm hold on their lances.

At any other time, thought Henry, he would have thrilled at the sight of the long row of knights, mounted on their panoplied chargers, their burnished armour gleaming in the sun. But here and now, with the unsuspecting dragon-pack about to meet its doom, Henry wished himself a thousand miles—or even years—away.

The line of knights sat motionless on their chargers. A faint breeze fluttered at the plumes on their gleaming helmets.

Arthur, sitting at the head of the Round Table company, wearing the sadly tattered coat-of-many-windows, turned in his saddle and glanced down his either side at the single line of knights on horseback.

"Sir Bedivere, Sir Lancelot and I will venture into the quarry and drive the evil brutes out into the clearing," he cried. "The remainder of you will tarry outside and, once we've forced them into the open, you will mount a frontal attack while Bedivere, Lancelot and myself harry them from behind. Is that understood?"

"Aye, my liege!" The cry went up along the line.

"Then let us go to it with a will, men!" continued the king. "And pray that we may rid our land of these last remaining beasts of hell!" With which, Arthur pulled Emily's brolly out from behind his saddle and waved it three times above his head. On the second wave, the faulty catch on the umbrella burst open yet again and the magic mushroom sprang up over Arthur's head.

A rousing cheer went up from the company of the Round Table.

"To chivalry, honour and the magic mushroom!" cried King Arthur.

"To chivalry, honour and the magic mushroom!" echoed all the knights.

Arthur glanced down at Henry who was hovering by his

horse's hindquarters. "You'd better lie low, lad, out of harm's way," he said. "You can't be too careful as far as these accursed beasts are concerned."

"But they aren't accursed anything! Anyway . . ." began Henry.

"For . . . ward!" ordered the king, cutting the boy short.

Henry watched, sadly, as the long line of mounted knights, with Arthur in the lead, urged their chargers forward at a walk, across the clearing and towards the quarry. The boy's hand went up to his face and he brushed away a tear. He still couldn't rid himself of the thought that it was partly his fault the dragons had been discovered. If only he'd been more careful. If only he'd made some attempt to cover up the tracks that he and the young dragon had left. If only he'd led the young dragon off in another direction, instead of allowing it to lead *him*. If only there was someone he could turn to for help. If only . . .

"Henry!" Someone was whispering to him behind his back. "*Henry!*" it went again, and: "*Pssssst!*"

He swung round and was astonished to see a familiar face peering at him from behind a tree.

"Hello, Mum," he said. "How did you get here?"

"Your friend Mr Merlin brought me."

Henry glanced around, puzzled. "Where is he? And how did he know where to look?"

The line of mounted knights was now halfway across the clearing and it was safe for Emily to come out of her hiding-place.

"Oh, that was easy-peasy," she said. "There's been so much rushing to and fro of knights between here and Camelot, it

would have been very difficult *not* to have found you. Merlin told us about how you were trying to save the dragons so we came to help."

"I'm afraid you got here too late," said Henry, glancing forlornly across at King Arthur and his Round Table Company who were drawing closer and closer to the quarry. Henry sighed and shrugged. "It doesn't make much difference anyway," he continued. "What could the three of us do against King Arthur and all his men?"

"You mean the *four* of us," said Emily. "Oh, but I was

forgetting—you don't know about the Great Alma, do you?"

"The Great *who*?" said Henry, puzzled. "And where *is* Merlin?"

"You'll see," said Emily, comfortably. She nodded towards the quarry. "Just watch," she added.

Henry followed her glance, more puzzled than before.

King Arthur drew up his charger and raised his right hand. Behind him, the line of knights reined in their mounts at his command. Then, signalling to Bedivere and Lancelot to do the same, he slid from his saddle to the ground.

"We three will go in on foot," announced Arthur. "It'll be easier that way for us to drive the foul beasts out. Once we've got them out here, in the open, we'll remount for the kill."

Bedivere and Lancelot nodded and, like Arthur, handed their horses' reins to one of their companions. They approached the quarry silently. Arthur carried the magic mushroom over his head with one hand and held his sword, Excalibur, in the other. Sir Bedivere and Sir Lancelot had also drawn their swords.

Over by the edge of the wood, Emily took note of Arthur's appearance for the first time and let out a little gasp of anger. "Well! I must say I like his cheek!" she said. "That's *my* brolly he's abducted—and just look at the state he's got my plastic mac in!"

Then, as Arthur and the two knights drew near to the cleft in the rocks which led into the quarry, a figure stepped out in front of them, barring the way.

"Get out of my way, you old fool!" hissed Arthur.

"Take heed, Arthur of Camelot!" said Merlin the Magician,

his quavering voice ringing out across the clearing. "Return from whence you came before it is too late!"

"Stand aside, you silly old meddler!" snapped Arthur. "Before I lose my temper! What do you think you're doing here anyway?"

"I have come to warn you, Arthur!" continued the old magician. "You must not destroy these creatures! To do so would be to incur the wrath of those that invoke the Forces of Magic!" And, to add weight to his words, Merlin waved his long thin fingers in the air, muttered one of his incantations, and produced a string of flags of all nations from his sleeve and a pot hen's egg from behind Arthur's ear.

Bedivere and Lancelot blinked in surprise and an appreciative murmur went up from the line of Round Table Knights. But Arthur was unimpressed.

"I've no time now for your conjuring tricks," snarled the king. "I'm telling you for the last time, Merlin, stand aside or suffer the consequences!"

"And I am also giving you one final warning," quavered the magician. "It is not I whose power you are questioning but She Who Is The Queen of All the Dragons."

"And who might that be?" demanded Arthur.

"The—er—The Great Alma," said Merlin, a trifle unsurely.

Arthur looked at Bedivere and Lancelot. "*Who* did he say?" he said with a frown. "Who's the Great Alma?"

Bedivere and Lancelot exchanged mystified glances and shook their heads.

"I've no idea," said Lancelot.

"Search me," said Bedivere.

"Ta-raaaAAA!" cried the Great Alma, appearing in person as if on cue from behind a rock. She had just succeeded, with the aid of Merlin's flint, in lighting a couple of torches fashioned out of straw and sticks. She now held a blazing torch in either hand. The sequins glittered on her frock. Her golden hair glowed in the sun. "I'm the Great Alma," she said, curtseying to King Arthur rather nervously.

King Arthur scowled. "It's one of those witches that we caught," he said. "What's she doing here? Why isn't she in the dungeon? Who let her out? If this is more of your trickery, Merlin—"

"Nay, sire," said Merlin, shaking his head firmly, "she sometimes takes on the *guise* of a witch—or even, on occasion, that of a frog or newt—but the dungeon has not been dug yet that is deep enough to hold her. In truth, your majesty, she is indeed the Queen of all the Dragons." He glanced across at the Great Alma and hissed at her under his breath, "Get on with it!"

The Great Alma curtseyed again and then began her fire-eating act for the benefit of the Round Table Company.

First of all, she lifted one of her burning torches and placed it in her mouth. An awed murmur went up from the line of knights and Bedivere and Lancelot exchanged a puzzled glance.

"Humph," grunted Arthur uneasily. "Is that *all* she does?"

The Great Alma tossed her golden curls and her sequinned frock twinkled in the sunlight. Then, taking the blazing torch out of her mouth, she lifted up the second burning brand and appeared to eat the flames from that one too.

"Oooooh!" gasped the line of mounted knights.

"Aaaaah!" gulped Sir Lancelot and Sir Bedivere.

King Arthur tried to hide the fact that he was shivering slightly.

The Great Alma opened her mouth and blew. A bright gold-and-orange tongue of flame burst out of the Great Alma's mouth and singed the grass.

The line of chargers whinnied and bucked and reared in fright while their riders hid their faces.

"Truly she breathes the fiery breath of a dragon!" moaned Sir Lancelot, dropping to his knees and clasping his hands above his head.

"Verily she is more dragon than wench!" groaned Sir Bedivere, falling full-length to the ground and covering his head with his hands.

"It's . . . it's trickery, I tell you," stuttered King Arthur. "The . . . the witch holds no fears as far as I . . ." But his voice trailed away and he held up the magic mushroom for protection as the Great Alma walked towards him. "What do you want of me, Great Alma?" he muttered tremulously.

"Can I borrow your sword for a minute?" asked the Great Alma.

"Do you promise me I'll get it back?" said King Arthur.

The Great Alma nodded and took the bejewelled Excalibur out of Arthur's nerveless fingers. Then, as the assembled company watched in terror, she threw back her head, lifted the gleaming blade with both of her hands, and slowly began to lower it down her throat.

The long low wail of horror that went up from the band of knights was awful in its intensity.

"Stop that!" cried the king. "Stop it this instant!" But the Great Alma paid not the slightest attention and Excalibur continued to disappear, centimetre by centimetre, down her throat. "Please, Merlin!" begged the king. "Do make her stop! That's my Excalibur! I pulled that sword out of a stone when nobody else could shift it! I'll be in all kinds of trouble if I don't get it back!"

"And if I *do* make her stop?" said Merlin.

"Oh, anything!" pleaded the king. "Just get it back, safe and sound, and I'll do anything you ask!"

"What about the dragons?" said the old magician.

"Oh, hang the dragons!" burbled Arthur. "The dragons can go free. Guinevere would have given me hell if I'd taken back more dragon-heads anyway."

"Do you swear the dragons shall come to no harm—ever?"

"Yes—yes!" said King Arthur, nodding briskly.

"Then swear it on the honour of the Round Table."

By this time, there was very little of Excalibur's blade showing above the Great Alma's open mouth.

"I swear it! I swear it!" cried Arthur. "Anything you ask! I swear it on the honour of the Round Table!"

Merlin nodded at the Great Alma who, hand over hand, retrieved Excalibur from her throat. "There you are, your majesty," she said, giving Arthur a reassuring smile as she handed him back his sword. "No harm done—I think you'll find it's just as good as new."

"Thanks very much," said Arthur gratefully.

"And while we're on the subject of returning borrowed articles," said Emily Hollins who had arrived on the scene with Henry while all this was taking place, "I'll thank you for the return of my plastic mackintosh."

"P-p-p-plastic mackin—what?" stuttered Arthur, wondering where the second witch had sprung from and also what she was talking about.

"She means the coat-of-many-windows, majesty," said Merlin.

"And I'll also thank you, your majesty, for my brolly if you've finished with it."

"B-b-b-brolly?" said the king.

"She is referring to the magic mushroom, my liege," said Merlin.

Arthur's face fell. "Aren't I to be allowed to keep *anything*?" he said. "I am the king when all's said and done!"

"Oh, very well—go on then," said Emily, generously. "You can have the brolly. I was thinking about buying a new one anyway. Just so long as you keep your promise about the dragons."

"Coming back to the subject of the dragons," said Arthur, glancing across towards the quarry where, as if sensing a new-won safety, an inquisitive snout had emerged and was sniffing the air, "we shall have to do *something* about them, you know."

"You gave your word you wouldn't harm them," protested Merlin. "You swore on the honour of the Round Table."

"I know! I know!" snapped Arthur, testily. "And I am a man of my word. All the same, we can't allow a whole pack of them to roam about at will—ravaging the countryside and terrorizing the peasants."

"They don't ravage anything," Henry put in hastily, and added, "or terrorize anybody either."

Arthur frowned at this unwelcome interruption. "When I require the opinion of a dud magician's boy-assistant, I shall ask for it," he said. "All right, I agree, they don't actually *ravage* anything," he continued, calming down. "But they do trample down vegetable patches—and steal cabbages from them without so much as a by-your-leave. They have *enormous* appetites. And it's all very well for you to say that they don't terrorize people—perhaps they *don't* mean any harm—but how would you like it, if you were an old peasant-woman and one of them stuck his snout in at your kitchen window in the middle of the afternoon?"

"You gave your word," repeated Merlin, firmly.

"I know! I know! And a king's word is as good as his bond. All I'm saying is that they can't be allowed the freedom of the kingdom. We'll have to do *something* about the brutes."

"I've got an idea if you'll only listen," said Henry.

"I've told you already, lad," snapped Arthur, "when I want the opinion of—"

"The least you can do is hear the boy out," said Merlin, cutting the king short.

"Oh, all right," said Arthur, relenting slightly. "What's this idea then, boy?"

"Well—" began Henry, as King Arthur settled down to listen.

Queen Guinevere and Arthur, the king, were standing on the

topmost battlements at Camelot looking down over the turreted parapet. They watched and listened as the two white swans squawked angrily and flapped their wings at a young dragon that had invaded their territory beside the moat.

Guinevere shaded her eyes against the sun and peered out across the greensward where more of the dragons were ambling about, nibbling at the short, sweet grass and munching leaves from the lower branches of the trees. Away off in the distance, the queen could just make out the figures of the Knights of the Round Table who were busily employed putting up a fence around Camelot's parkland.

"What did you say it was to be called?" she said to Arthur.

"If memory serves me correct, my love, the magician's young assistant referred to it as a Safari Park," said Arthur.

"What an odd name!" said Guinevere, wrinkling her brow. "Still, I'm sure they look more attractive wandering about the grounds than stuffed and mounted in the Great Hall. But are you sure we can afford to keep them?"

"That lad of Merlin's suggested that we make the peasants pay to come in and see them."

"Why should the peasants give us money to come and look at dragons when they've been running away from them most of their lives?"

"I don't know, dear," said Arthur. "But the magician's assistant seemed to think they would. He struck me as being a bright young lad. He also seemed to think we could charge the peasants a bit extra and let them look over the castle."

"Who on earth, in their right minds, would pay good money to gaze at this old ruin?"

"I don't know that either," said Arthur. "But the second witch, the one who gave me the magic mushroom, suggested we could charge them even more money for cream-teas."

"What's a cream-tea?" asked the queen.

"I'm afraid that's something else I don't know, dear," admitted Arthur.

"It seems to me that you don't know very much about anything, Arthur."

"True enough, dear," said the king. "But as I understood it, from the way the witch and the magician's assistant explained things, it's all to do with something known as Visiting Stately Homes."

"It doesn't sound to me," said Guinevere coldly, "like something that will catch on." She crossed to the flight of stone steps where she paused for a last word before setting off down to her chamber. "Oh, and by the way, I'm afraid it will be cold peacocks' tongues again for dinner—we're still eating up leftovers from that last feast you insisted on having."

Arthur sighed. He felt inside his robes and, to cheer himself up, took out the small going-away present that the witch-with-the-coat-of-many-windows had given him. It was a half-empty tube of Exceedingly Strong Peppermints. He popped one into his mouth. A moment later he pulled a face and spat the peppermint out again. The small round mint flew over the parapet and fell down, down, down into the moat.

King Arthur fanned at his mouth with his hand.

10

"It's time for you to go," said Merlin from the door of his cave. "You'll need to change back into your ordinary clothes."

"I shan't be a minute," said Henry, stroking the snout of the young dragon. The creature, which had grown quite fond of Henry, had frisked across to bid him goodbye.

The old magician strolled over and stood by the boy and the beast.

The young dragon was nuzzling up against Henry's jerkin and the boy felt something pressing his side. He put his hand in his pocket and took out the small leather bottle which Merlin had given him . . . when? Had it only been a day ago? The young dragon panted with excitement. Its long pink tongue shot out and licked frenziedly at the top of the bottle. Henry took out the stopper and tipped the green mixture into the creature's mouth. The dragon licked Henry's hand and slapped its tail against the ground.

"*That's* what it is!" said Henry, laughing. "Dragon-food."

Merlin smiled. "I shall brew up a cauldron of it for them every night."

"How long will they survive for now?" asked Henry, stroking the young dragon's leathery neck and tugging, playfully, at the loose folds of skin beneath its ear.

The old magician shook his head. "Who can tell?" he said. "I'm afraid they're still a dying species—but they'll certainly be around much longer than they would have been without your help. The world will be a sadder place when they are gone."

Henry nodded.

A cloud passed over the sun.

"You really must be going, you know," said the old magician.

"Yes." The boy gave the beast a last long lingering pat. "Goodbye, Draggie," he said. "Take care of yourself."

Emily Hollins and the Great Alma were waiting for Henry inside Merlin's cave.

"I *have* enjoyed myself," said Emily, as Henry changed into his everyday clothes.

"Me too," said the Great Alma enthusiastically. "It's been smashing! Except that dungeon, of course. That wasn't very nice. But even that will be something to remember, won't it, in the years to come?"

Merlin shook his head. "I'm afraid you won't remember anything," he said. "The moment that you step out of the Time Tunnel, you'll forget everything that's happened here."

"Every little thing?" asked Emily, sadly.

"Every single solitary incident."

"Oh well, never mind." Emily brightened up. "Perhaps it's all for the best. Nobody would ever have believed us anyway."

"I'm ready," said Henry.

The three visitors to Camelot crossed to the back of the cave

128

and the entrance to the long, dark tunnel.

"Goodbye," said Merlin. "I don't suppose we'll ever see each other again."

"Aren't you coming with us?" asked Henry.

Merlin shook his head.

"But what about your magic cabinet?"

"The magic cabinet will take care of itself," said the old magician.

Emily and the Great Alma waved goodbye to Merlin and stepped into the tunnel.

Henry moved to follow them and then a thought occurred to him. "What *time* will it be when we get back?" he asked.

"Why—precisely the same time as when you left," said Merlin. "When else?"

Although he had been the last one to enter the Time Tunnel, Henry Hollins was the first to step out of the magic cabinet on to the stage of the Pier Theatre, Cockleton-on-Sea. Coming out of total blackness, Henry blinked at the bright stage lighting which shone down on him from all angles.

The theatre audience cheered and clapped.

"That was a good trick, wasn't it?" said Albert Hollins, turning to the seat next to him. But, to his surprise, he realized that Emily wasn't there. He was even more astonished when, turning his attention back to the stage, Albert saw his wife follow his son out of the magician's magic cabinet. How on earth did she get in there, he wondered?

The audience roared with laughter. They had seen a small boy enter the box, disappear, and now here he was returning with a plump lady determinedly clutching her handbag. Up on the stage, Emily tried to get her bearings. A moment before she had been sitting in the third row of the stalls. Now, all at once, she appeared to be part of the entertainment.

Before Emily Hollins could collect her thoughts, the Great Alma stepped out of the magic cabinet.

The audience stamped its feet and whistled through its fingers.

The Great Alma curtseyed. She had no idea what she was doing there but she had spent a lifetime in the theatre and knew how to appreciate applause when it came her way. The Great Alma curtseyed for a second time.

The theatre manager, Mr Grundy, was watching from the wings. "What the blue blazes is going on?" he demanded of the man who worked the curtains.

"No idea, guv."

On the stage, Emily Hollins and Henry were still gazing around while the Great Alma was curtseying for a third time.

"Where's that old fool of a magician?" snapped the theatre manager.

"Dunno, guv," said the man who worked the curtains.

"Ring down the curtain," said the theatre manager.

The audience clapped and clapped until its hands ached as the red plush curtain came down and the Great Alma managed to get in one last curtsey.

The theatre manager shook his head in disbelief. "Get hold of an attendant," he said to the man who worked the curtains, "and see that those two members of the audience are taken safely back to their seats." Then, as the Great Alma came off stage he said to her, "I'm glad your throat's better. You can go on in the second half instead of that ridiculous magician."

"What magician?" asked the Great Alma, wondering which sore throat the manager was talking about.

"The *old* magician," said the theatre manager, "the one who did the trick with that magic cabinet over —" He broke off as he glanced towards the stage.

The magic cabinet had vanished completely.

When the final curtain came down on the matinée performance, Emily Hollins turned to her husband, Albert. "I thoroughly enjoyed every minute of that," she said. "It was what I call an afternoon well spent."

"Same here," said Albert. "What did you think of it, Henry?"

"Smashing," said their son. "I thought that lady sword-swallower was terrific."

"That's funny," said Emily. "I was sure I put my brolly under the seat when we arrived. It's disappeared."

"You'd lose your head if it wasn't fastened on," said Albert, winking at Henry.

"And just look at this!" said Emily, unfolding her see-through raincoat. "It's full of holes. How did that happen?"

"Moths," said Albert.

"Moths don't go for plastic," said Emily. They had moved into the theatre's centre aisle and were following the rest of the audience towards the exit-doors at the back. "What am I going to do," asked Emily, "if it's pelting cats and dogs outside?"

"I bet it isn't!" said Henry Hollins. "I bet the sun's out."

"Let's hope it is," said Albert. "It's only half past four. If it isn't raining, we can get in a game of beach-cricket before we start to think about tea."

"My turn to bowl," said Henry. "Mum's turn to field, your turn to bat. I hope it isn't raining." He crossed his fingers. "I hope the sun's blazing down like mad!"

It was.

Other great reads ⤙ *from* **Red Fox**

Further Red Fox titles that you might enjoy reading are listed on the following pages. They are available in bookshops or they can be ordered directly from us.

If you would like to order books, please send this form and the money due to:

ARROW BOOKS, BOOKSERVICE BY POST, PO BOX 29, DOUGLAS, ISLE OF MAN, BRITISH ISLES. Please enclose a cheque or postal order made out to Arrow Books Ltd for the amount due, plus 75p per book for postage and packing to a maximum of £7.50, both for orders within the UK. For customers outside the UK, please allow £1.00 per book.

NAME_____

ADDRESS_____

_____

Please print clearly.

Whilst every effort is made to keep prices low, it is sometimes necessary to increase cover prices at short notice. If you are ordering books by post, to save delay it is advisable to phone to confirm the correct price. The number to ring is THE SALES DEPARTMENT 071 (if outside London) 973 9700.

Other great reads ⤺ *from* **Red Fox**

Enter the gripping world of the REDWALL series

A bestselling series based around Redwall Abbey, the home of a community of peace-loving mice. The first book, REDWALL, was nominated for the Carnegie Award.

REDWALL   Brian Jacques

As the mice of Redwall Abbey prepare for a feast, Cluny, the evil one-eyed rat, prepares for battle!

0 09 951200 9   £4.50

MOSSFLOWER   Brian Jacques

The gripping tale of how Redwall Abbey was established through the bravery of the legendary mouse Martin.

0 09 955400 3   £4.50

MATTIMEO   Brian Jacques

Slagar the fox is intent on revenge and plans to bring death and destruction to Redwall, particularly Matthias mouse.

0 09 967540 4   £4.50

MARIEL OF REDWALL   Brian Jacques

The start of the second Redwall trilogy with the adventures of a young mousemaid, Mariel.

0 09 992960 0   £4.50

SALAMANDASTRON   Brian Jacques

Redwall is in trouble! Feragho the Assassin is attacking the fortress of Salamandastron and Dryditch Fever approaches . . .

0 09 914361 5   £4.50

MARTIN THE WARRIOR   Brian Jacques

Badrang the tyrant stoat, has forced captive slaves to build his fortress, but a young mouse, Martin, plots a daring escape.

0 09 928171 6   £4.50

BESTSELLING FICTION FROM RED FOX

☐ The Present Takers	Aidan Chambers	£2.99
☐ Battle for the Park	Colin Dann	£2.99
☐ Orson Cart Comes Apart	Steve Donald	£1.99
☐ The Last Vampire	Willis Hall	£2.99
☐ Harvey Angell	Diana Hendry	£2.99
☐ Emil and the Detectives	Erich Kästner	£2.99
☐ Krindlekrax	Philip Ridley	£2.99

PRICES AND OTHER DETAILS ARE LIABLE TO CHANGE

ARROW BOOKS, BOOKSERVICE BY POST, PO BOX 29, DOUGLAS, ISLE OF MAN, BRITISH ISLES

NAME ....

ADDRESS ....

....

....

Please enclose a cheque or postal order made out to B.S.B.P. Ltd. for the amount due and allow the following for postage and packing:

U.K. CUSTOMERS: Please allow 75p per book to a maximum of £7.50

B.F.P.O. & EIRE: Please allow 75p per book to a maximum of £7.50

OVERSEAS CUSTOMERS: Please allow £1.00 per book.

While every effort is made to keep prices low it is sometimes necessary to increase cover prices at short notice. Arrow Books reserve the right to show new retail prices on covers which may differ from those previously advertised in the text or elsewhere.

BESTSELLING FICTION FROM RED FOX

BESTSELLING FICTION FROM RED FOX

☐ Blood	Alan Durant	£3.50
☐ Tina Come Home	Paul Geraghty	£3.50
☐ Del-Del	Victor Kelleher	£3.50
☐ Paul Loves Amy Loves Christo	Josephine Poole	£3.50
☐ If It Weren't for Sebastian	Jean Ure	£3.50
☐ You'll Never Guess the End	Barbara Wersba	£3.50
☐ The Pigman	Paul Zindel	£3.50

PRICES AND OTHER DETAILS ARE LIABLE TO CHANGE

ARROW BOOKS, BOOKSERVICE BY POST, PO BOX 29, DOUGLAS, ISLE OF MAN, BRITISH ISLES

NAME...

ADDRESS..

....

....

Please enclose a cheque or postal order made out to B.S.B.P. Ltd. for the amount due and allow the following for postage and packing:

U.K. CUSTOMERS: Please allow 75p per book to a maximum of £7.50

B.F.P.O. & EIRE: Please allow 75p per book to a maximum of £7.50

OVERSEAS CUSTOMERS: Please allow £1.00 per book.

While every effort is made to keep prices low it is sometimes necessary to increase cover prices at short notice. Arrow Books reserve the right to show new retail prices on covers which may differ from those previously advertised in the text or elsewhere.

Other great reads from **Red Fox**

Have a chuckle with Red Fox Fiction!

FLOSSIE TEACAKE'S FUR COAT   Hunter Davies

Flossie just wants to be grown-up, like her big sister
Bella – and when she tries on the mysterious fur coat
she finds in Bella's bedroom, her wildest dreams come
true . . .
ISBN 0 09 996710 3   £2.99

SNOTTY BUMSTEAD   Hunter Davies

Snotty's mum has gone away leaving him with lots of
cash and the house to himself! Burgers for breakfast,
football in the front room – and no homework! But
can he keep the nosey grown-ups away?
ISBN 0 09 997710 9   £2.99

HENRY HOLLINS AND THE DINOSAUR
Willis Hall

Little did Henry think, when he found the fossilized
egg at the seaside, that it was actually a fossilized
DINOSAUR egg! He had even less idea that it would
be no time at all before he would be travelling up the
moorway on a dinosaur's back!
ISBN 0 09 911611 1   £2.99

THE LAST VAMPIRE   Willis Hall

The Hollins family are on holiday in Europe, and all
goes well until they stay the night in a spooky castle,
miles from nowhere. Even worse, they discover that
they are in the castle belonging to Count Alucard.
ISBN 0 09 911541 7   £2.99

TRIV IN PURSUIT   Michael Coleman

One by one, the teachers at St Ethelred's School are
vanishing, leaving cryptic notes behind. "Triv"
Trevellyan smells something fishy going on and is
determined to find out just what is happening!
ISBN 0 09 991660 6   £2.99

Action-Packed Drama with Red Fox Fiction!

SIMPLE SIMON Yvonne Coppard

Simon isn't stupid – he's just not very good at practical things. So when Mum collapses, it's Cara, his younger sister who calls the ambulance and keeps a cool head. Simon plans to show what he can do too, in a crisis, but his plan goes frighteningly wrong . . .
ISBN 0 09 910531 4 £2.99

LOW TIDE William Mayne

Winner of the Guardian Children's Fiction Award.

The low tide at Jade Bay leaves fish on dry land and a wreck high on a rock. Is this the treasure ship the divers have been looking for? Three friends vow to find out – and find themselves swept away into adventure.
ISBN 0 09 918311 0 £3.50

THE INTRUDER John Rowe Townsend

It isn't often that you meet someone who claims to be you. But that's what happens to Arnold Haithwaite. The real Arnold has to confront the menacing intruder before he takes over his life completely.
ISBN 0 09 999260 4 £3.50

GUILTY Ruth Thomas

Everyone in Kate's class says that the local burglaries have been done by Desmond Locke's dad, because he's just come out of prison. Kate and Desmond think otherwise and set out to prove who really is *guilty*.
ISBN 0 09 918591 1 £2.99

Other great reads *from* **Red Fox**

Leap into humour and adventure with Joan Aiken

Joan Aiken writes wild adventure stories laced with comedy and melodrama that have made her one of the best-known writers today. Her James III series, which begins with *The Wolves of Willoughby Chase*, has been recognized as a modern classic. Packed with action from beginning to end, her books are a wild romp through a history that never happened.

THE WOLVES OF WILLOUGHBY CHASE
ISBN 0 09 997250 6   £2.99

BLACK HEARTS IN BATTERSEA
ISBN 0 09 988860 2   £3.50

NIGHT BIRDS ON NANTUCKET
ISBN 0 09 988890 4   £3.50

THE STOLEN LAKE
ISBN 0 09 988840 8   £3.50

THE CUCKOO TREE
ISBN 0 09 988870 X   £3.50

DIDO AND PA
ISBN 0 09 988850 5   £3.50

IS
ISBN 0 09 910921 2   £2.99

THE WHISPERING MOUNTAIN
ISBN 0 09 988830 0   £3.50

MIDNIGHT IS A PLACE
ISBN 0 09 979200 1   £3.50

THE SHADOW GUESTS
ISBN 0 09 988820 3   £2.99

Other great reads <from *Red Fox*

Chocks Away with Biggles!

Red Fox are proud to reissue a collection of some of Captain W. E. Johns'
most exciting and fast-paced stories about the flying Ace, in brand-new
editions, guaranteed to entertain young and old readers alike.

BIGGLES LEARNS TO FLY
ISBN 0 09 999740 1 £3.50

BIGGLES IN FRANCE
ISBN 0 09 928311 5 £3.50

BIGGLES IN THE CAMELS ARE COMING
ISBN 0 09 928321 2 £3.50

BIGGLES AND THE RESCUE FLIGHT
ISBN 0 09 993860 X £3.50

BIGGLES OF THE FIGHTER SQUADRON
ISBN 0 09 993870 7 £3.50

BIGGLES FLIES EAST
ISBN 0 09 993780 8 £3.50

BIGGLES & CO.
ISBN 0 09 993800 6 £3.50

BIGGLES IN SPAIN
ISBN 0 09 913441 1 £3.50

BIGGLES DEFIES THE SWASTIKA
ISBN 0 09 993790 5 £3.50

BIGGLES IN THE ORIENT
ISBN 0 09 913461 6 £3.50

BIGGLES DEFENDS THE DESERT
ISBN 0 09 993840 5 £3.50

BIGGLES FAILS TO RETURN
ISBN 0 09 993850 2 £3.50

BIGGLES: SPITFIRE PARADE – a Biggles graphic novel
ISBN 0 09 930105 9 £3.99

Other great reads *from* **Red Fox**

Share the magic of The Magician's House by William Corlett

There is magic in the air from the first moment the three Constant children, William, Mary and Alice arrive at their uncle's house in the Golden Valley. But it's when they meet the Magician, William Tyler, and hear of the Great Task he has for them that the adventures really begin.

THE STEPS UP THE CHIMNEY

Evil threatens Golden House in its hour of need – and the Magician's animals come to the children's aid – but travelling with a fox brings its own dangers.

ISBN 0 09 985370 1 £2.99

THE DOOR IN THE TREE

William, Mary and Alice find a cruel and vicious sport threatening the peace of Golden Valley on their return to this magical place.

ISBN 0 09 997390 1 £2.99

THE TUNNEL BEHIND THE WATERFALL

Evil creatures mass against the children as they attempt to master time travel.

ISBN 0 09 997910 1 £2.99

THE BRIDGE IN THE CLOUDS

With the Magician seriously ill, it's up to the three children to complete the Great Task alone.

ISBN 0 09 918301 9 £2.99

Join the RED FOX Reader's Club

The Red Fox Reader's Club is for readers of all ages. All you have to do is ask your local bookseller or librarian for a Red Fox Reader's Club card. As an official Red Fox Reader you only have to borrow or buy eight Red Fox books in order to qualify for your own Red Fox Reader's Clubpack – full of exciting surprises! If you have any difficulty obtaining a Red Fox Reader's Club card please write to: Random House Children's Books Marketing Department, 20 Vauxhall Bridge Road, London SW1V 2SA.